THE

The Woman in the Moon

398

The Woman in the Moon
and other tales of forgotten heroines

James Riordan

Illustrated by
Angela Barrett

Hutchinson
London Sydney Auckland Johannesburg

To my daughter Natalie,
who helps me to understand

Copyright © Text James Riordan 1984
Copyright © Illustrations Angela Barrett 1984

First published in Great Britain in 1984 by
Hutchinson Children's Books Ltd
An imprint of The Random Century Group
20 Vauxhall Bridge Road
London SW1V 2SA

First published in paperback in 1990 by
Hutchinson Children's Books
An imprint of The Random Century Group Ltd
20 Vauxhall Bridge Road
London SW1V 2SA

Reprinted in 1992, 1993

Random Century Australia (Pty) Ltd
20 Alfred Street, Milsons Point, Sydney 2061, Australia

Random Century New Zealand Limited
32-34 View Road, PO Box 40 086, Glenfield, Auckland 10

Century Hutchinson South Africa (Pty) Ltd
PO Box 337, Bergvlei 2012, South Africa

Set in Linotron Baskerville by
Tradespools Ltd, Frome, Somerset

Printed in China

British Library Cataloguing in Publication Data is available.
ISBN 0 09 174078 9

Contents

Preface

Why are witches evil and ugly, yet sorcerers good?
Why do fairytales have wicked stepmothers, but hardly ever wicked stepfathers?

Why are there ugly sisters, but no ugly brothers?

Why are women in fairytales either hatching evil, or acting as prizes for men's adventures – like Snow White, Cinderella or Sleeping Beauty?

And why are most stories about boys, men and male animals?

Why indeed?

The irony is that the original storytellers were mostly women – and humble working women at that – who themselves led robust lives. That is why Charles Perrault called his stories 'old wives' tales'. Yet those who wrote down the stories were mainly men: Perrault, the Grimm Brothers, Joseph Jacobs, Andrew Lang and the rest. And when the tales came to be published, mainly in the last century, the characters were made to fit into society's ideas of the way men and women should behave.

The ideal hero had to be adventurous, brave, strong, daring and protective towards girls.

The ideal heroine had to be meek, gentle, helpless, inferior to boys in almost every way; and above all she had to be beautiful. And often her sole ambition was to marry a handsome prince!

Fairytales, therefore, portrayed boys and girls as society thought they *should* be, and not as they *could* be.

For a long time too there had been a fear of women, of their power and their wisdom. Hence the cruel burning of innocent old women as witches in the fifteenth and sixteenth centuries, and the use of witches in fairytale to scare little children and make them obedient.

Does it matter? Surely no one takes fairytales seriously? Well, do they? Children learn a lot about the world through children's literature generally, about other girls and boys – how they talk, act and feel, what is expected of them, and what they can be when they grow up.

So fairytales play an important part in the early development of ideas, simply because they are so popular. They feature in comics and films, and are read over and over again by parents and teachers whom children trust above all others, and they are usually among the first stories and films that children come upon.

This is a collection of folk tales from around the world. Some I have gathered on my wanderings through foreign countries, others I have translated and retold. These stories feature heroines who are central characters in their own right; they are not defined in terms of men. And just as the usual collections of tales featuring heroes are not meant for boys alone, so this book is meant for girls *and* boys, and for their parents and teachers. For the price of stereotyping in stories is not paid by girls alone. Not all boys wish to be adventurous, tough and aggressive. Some want to be homeloving, gentle and caring – qualities some people define as feminine.

So here, for a change – a drop in the ocean – are some stories of bold and strong and clever heroines who break the magic spell of fairytale; stories that may help girls and boys to feel free to be themselves; stories of mutual respect and dignity, cooperation and friendship.

After all, stories can and should encourage the imagination and creativity of all children – at the expense of none.

The Woman in the Moon

An Indian tale from North America. The 'big water'
in the story is Lake Superior

Many snows in the past, before the White Man came to take the Indian lands, the Chippewa were great and strong. They were as many as leaves upon the maple tree; their tents were as thick as the stars up in the sky. They were feared by their foes and loved by their friends. The Good Spirit smiled upon the People; and the People were content.

In those long-ago years, on the shores of the big water there lived an Indian maid, Lone Bird. She was the only child of She Eagle and Dawn of Day. And no daughter of the tribe was so proud and strong as she. From all the camps of the Chippewa nation young braves would come to seek her favour. But she stared coolly at them all. In vain they sang to her of their skill as hunters, of their daring in war. In vain they brought gifts to the lodge of She Eagle and Dawn of Day.

The maiden's heart was, they said, like winter's ice.

Her father tried to breathe some warmth into his daughter's heart. He praised the skill and courage of the braves he knew; he told her that no maid of the tribe had so noble a band of suitors from whom to choose.

But Lone Bird took his hand in hers. She smiled as she said, 'Do I not have my parents' love? What need have I to wed?'

Dawn of Day made no reply. He did not understand. How could he? Next day he went from his lodge, summoned young braves of the camp and told them of his plan.

'All you who want my daughter as your squaw should gather on the shore. A race will be run. He who is fleetest of foot shall have her as prize.'

At these words, the young men's hearts were filled with joy. Each eagerly made ready for the race; and each hoped for the deer's nimbleness of foot.

News of the contest spread through the Chippewa camps, and braves came from far and near. On the morning of the race, a great throng gathered upon the shore.

The elders were there to strut and judge the race.

Mothers were there to give comfort to their sons and cast an eye on future brides.

Fathers came to seek sons worthy of their daughters.

Daughters were there to see the braves and be noticed in return.

And, of course, the braves were there, painted in the finest hues and plumed with feathers of the eagle and the turkey cock.

Only one member of the tribe was missing – Lone Bird. She sat in her parents' lodge alone, in tears.

When all was ready for the race, the braves lined up, bronze muscles rippling in the sun and hearts pounding like war drums. At the signal, they all dashed forward in a jostling throng.

Soon two runners had broken free of the chasing pack. They were Bending Bow and Hunter of Deer. Both had loved Lone Bird for many moons. Each was as fleet-footed as a deer, as swift as the rushing wind. Neither could outstrip the other, and when they reached the finishing line, the judges could not tell which brave had won.

So Bending Bow and Hunter of Deer raced again. And once more they came in side by side. A third time they ran, and no victor was declared.

'Let them jump against each other,' someone said.

Only one member of the tribe was missing

Yet when they jumped, neither could beat the other by a hair.

'Let them display their hunting skill,' the elders declared.

So next day at dawn, Bending Bow and Hunter of Deer set off across the plain. On their return, each threw down the skins of ten bears and twenty wolves.

The elders muttered amongst themselves and an anxious buzz went round the tribe: it was clear that the Good Spirit had been at work. Lone Bird's father, Dawn of Day, returned to his lodge with a troubled mind. There sat his daughter, head bowed, eyes red with weeping, knuckles white upon trembling hands. His heart was moved, for he dearly loved his only child.

Lifting her head, he spoke gently to her. 'You must not weep, daughter. Every man must have a wife, every wife a man.'

'Dear Father,' she replied, 'but what if I do not wish it to be so?'

Sadly he returned to the elders gathered beside the lake.

'The race is at an end,' he said. 'Bending Bow and Hunter of Deer have done well; but it seems the Good Spirit's will is against our plan. My daughter shall remain unwed.'

And so, dismayed, the braves returned to their camps.

Summers passed; leaves of autumn fell; cold winter winds blew across the lake. And then one spring, as the snows began to melt, Dawn of Day went to Maple-Syrup Hill to make sugar from the sap of maple trees. As always, Lone Bird went along to gather the sweet liquid in birch-bark bowls. By and by, as smoke was curling slowly from her father's fire, she sat upon a rock and glanced around. The sun was warm and bright, the air was filled with the scent of fir and pine; yet somehow Lone Bird felt sad. Her thoughts were of her parents, of their silver hair and stumbling steps; their journey to the spirits was not far off.

'What will become of me when they are gone?' she thought. 'I have no brother or sister, no children of my own, no one to share my tent.'

And for the first time she felt the chill hand of loneliness grip her heart. As she gazed down the slope at the early snowdrops, pushing their frail heads through the margin of the snow, she saw that they grew in clusters, like small families. As she watched the birds busily building nests, she saw that they too did not live alone. Just then she heard the whirring of a flock of wild geese swooping across the lake; they landed in a furrow upon the water and glided away in pairs.

'No flowers, no birds, not even wild geese live alone,' she murmured to herself.

Her lonely thoughts made her sadder still. She recalled her coolness to the braves who used to court her; no longer did they come. She recalled her father's efforts to find her a husband; he had long since let her be.

'Yet still I am glad I did not wed,' she sighed. 'No one understands that I have no love in my heart for men.'

For a long time she sat upon the rock above the lake, wrapped in her gloomy thoughts. When she rose to go it was already dusk and the full round moon made a silvery path across the lake. Lone Bird gazed up longingly at the bright moon in the sky and, stretching forth her arms, she cried, 'Oh, how beautiful you are. If only I had you to love, I would not be lonely.'

The Good Spirit heard the cry of the lonely maid and carried her up to the moon.

Meanwhile, her father finished his work upon the slopes and, not seeing her anywhere about, he went back home. Yet when he did not find her in the lodge he returned to Maple-Syrup Hill. From there he called his daughter's name. 'Lone Bird! Lone Bird!'

Time and again he called.

No answer came.

His worried eyes searched the trees, the slopes, the surface of the lake. Then in despair he looked up to the sky towards the brightly shining moon. Could it be? Yes, there was no doubt. He clearly saw his daughter smiling down, held in the moon's pale arms.

She seemed to say she was content.

No longer did he grieve. No longer did She Eagle or Dawn of Day worry about their daughter's fate. They knew she would be cared for tenderly by the loving moon.

Many, many snows have passed since the days of Lone Bird and her

Chippewa tribe. Their people have become weak and few; their tents are scattered to the winds. White strangers occupy their hunting grounds and the graves of their dead go unmourned.

But the flowers still bloom in springtime; birds still build their nests; wild geese fly and stars still shine. And if you look up to the moon, you can still see the face of Lone Bird smiling down. She gives hope to her people as they tell her story by their fading fires.

She understands. And so do they.

A Mother's Yarn

A Saami story from Lappland in the Arctic Circle

Long, long ago, there lived a woman and her husband with their daughter Nastai.

The old man was a simple soul who did what he was told. Not that he minded at all, for what he was not told he did not think of by himself. The mistress, though, had all her wits about her and there was little she could not do or did not know.

She was very patient with the old man and would say, 'Come on, old-timer, we need fresh meat.' Then she would take a bow and arrows, and lead the way into the forest.

Or she would say, 'Come along, Grandad, we need some fish.' And she would launch the boat herself, take up the oars and row out to the middle of the lake; she would cast the nets and they would haul in the fish together.

The family lived and prospered, with meat and fish, fur coats and feather beds. Meanwhile, Nastai was growing up and learning all her mother knew. When she was big enough to help, the family lived even better than before.

But one day, bad times fell upon the old pair – a sickness swept the land and laid its hand upon them. In time, the old man survived, but the mistress did not recover. Before she died, she called Nastai to her.

'I am dying, Daughter. I must leave the old man in your care. See you treat him well.' And with that she breathed her last.

Nastai kept her word. She made her father cranberry tea, rubbed bear fat into his skin and gave him venison liver to make him strong. Soon he was fit and well.

Word now went round the camps that the wise woman was dead, leaving the daughter and the old man alone in the cosy house. In time the news reached a distant camp in which there lived a beggarwoman and her daughter. Winds had torn holes in their mud-baked hut, their cooking pots leaked, their fishing nets were rotten, their harpoons broken. But they did not care. They had an old buck deer, and when they wanted food they would hitch him to a sledge and ride from camp to camp to beg for meat. No one would turn them away; such was the custom while folk had food.

When the beggarwoman heard of the old widower, she drove her sledge over plain and hill until she reached his house. How pleased she was to see a herd of reindeer grazing, well-fed dogs running free and the old man sitting outside his cosy home.

'Are you the widower with the herd of deer?' she said.

He nodded.

'Then mind this: I'm now mistress here.'

The old man stared.

Nastai had gone for wood and was not at home. When she returned she was surprised to hear strange noises coming from the house. Opening the door, she saw a ragged woman wailing a song with a younger girl. Meanwhile, the old man was banging a spoon upon an empty pot, giggling like an oaf and dribbling down his chin. On the table stood an empty sealskin bag for fire water.

'What's this, Father,' Nastai said quietly, 'do we have guests?'

'Hold your tongue, girl!' shouted the beggarwoman. 'I'm no guest in my own house. I'm mistress here. Is that not so, old man?'

What could he say? His head fell forward in an unwilling nod.

Nastai did as she was told. She brought food at once: cloudberry preserve and fresh-baked rusks. She made up a feather bed and covered it with furs. Meanwhile, the two strangers crammed their mouths with food, before flopping down on the bed to sleep. All the time the old woman wondered how she would rid herself of Nastai.

It was barely light when the beggarwoman awoke. At once she ordered the old man to harness a team of reindeer and load all his fortune on a sledge.

'But your good-for-nothing daughter can stay here in her mother's hut,' she yelled. 'The three of us will live in plenty in my land.'

Meekly, the old man harnessed all his reindeer to a sledge and began to load it with furs and lace, reindeer hides and feather mattresses, fox and squirrel pelts, axes and harpoons. The two women packed the rest.

Not a crust of bread, not a scrap of meat was left; no fish, no hides, no covers to keep Nastai warm at night. It was cold and dark in the empty hut, and she was hungry. How was she to live? She sat upon the floor and sobbed as if her heart would break.

All of a sudden, she seemed to hear her mother's voice.

'Look about you, Nastai.'

She glanced around, searched high and low, but found nothing but a twist of yarn upon the floor. Yes, she remembered now: whenever her mother spun some yarn, she would tear off the thread and drop it on the floor. Nastai now picked it up and once more heard the voice.

'Nastai, remember what I taught you.'

She did remember.

Making a loop of yarn out of the thread, she ran to the forest, to a leafy glade where partridges often came to feed on berries. She put her loop on the ground and covered it in leaves. Long and patiently she waited; but at last she snared a lone, lame bird.

She took it home, stripped the veins from the bird's two legs and made another noose.

This time she caught two partridges in her traps. She plucked the feathers from the birds and now had meat for broth. But what could she make it in? She had neither pot, nor fire upon the hearth.

Again a voice was heard.

'Come now, Nastai, remember what I taught you.'

Back went the girl into the forest to seek a sturdy silver birch. When she found the right one, she began to tear off strips of bark.

These she took home and plaited into a bowl, which she coated with clay and left to dry out in the sun. And so she made a bark-clay pot.

Next she scooped up some water in her pot, dropped the partridges in and hung it on two sticks above the hearth. Already she had prepared dry moss, fir cones and twigs for a fire. Now she took two flint stones and struck them together. Thus she worked away until she raised a spark that lit the moss.

Soon the fire blazed; water boiled merrily in the pot and the partridges gave off a delicious smell. Nastai drank the broth and ate the meat, then went to set her traps again.

With each day that passed she caught more birds than ever; she fed on their meat, made traps out of their veins and stored up the feathers and the down. A whole heap of feathers grew up in the corner of the hut and, at night, she slept snug and warm inside. The only trouble was they got into her nose and mouth, making her cough and sneeze.

Then she recalled how her mother had spun some yarn into an eiderdown.

Off she went into the forest again, brought back a strong smooth stick and began to spin a thread from the down and veins; this she wound about the pole, just like a distaff. She spun the yarn and wove herself a cover which she filled with down and feathers. Placing white moss and grass upon the floor, she lay her eiderdown upon it. It was now clean and cosy inside the hut, the hearth fire blazed and meat simmered in the pot. All was well.

As time went by, however, she longed for company. It was then she seemed to hear her mother's voice again.

'Remember, Nastai, what I taught you.'

That gave her an idea.

Off she went into the forest, pulled up a stripling pine and broke off the roots. She plaited them with yarn and wove herself a strong lasso. That done, she walked for many days across the plain until she spied a reindeer herd. Hiding in the long white grass, downwind from the herd, she waited patiently. Presently, a little fawn strayed from a doe and wandered towards the clump of grass where Nastai was hiding. All at once, Nastai threw her lasso neatly about the fawn's neck, pulled it towards her and led it home.

She began to tend the fawn, feeding it with moss and grass, and giving it water to drink. The deer soon lost its fear and ran behind her as if she were the mother doe. And she put by some fodder for the fawn, with dry grass and moss, ready for the winter.

Then her thoughts turned to herself, for she had no food put by, no warm coat, no hat, no boots to wear. Again came her mother's voice.

'Nastai, remember what I taught you.'

This time she went down to the lake where there was a willow tree. She snapped off a branch, bent it into a bow and stretched her lasso across both ends. The bow was tough and springy. She then gathered a bundle of smooth sticks, dried them above the hearth and drove sharp flints into the ends.

Winter snow began to fall.

Nastai tethered the fawn close by her hut and went in search of food. She came upon some squirrels hopping along branches, nibbling fir cones; then she spotted a silver fox slinking across the snow, hunting mice. Taking careful aim, she loosed her arrows, killing a squirrel and the fox. She dragged her booty home, where she skinned the two animals, cleaned the furs and hung them up to dry.

Next day she went hunting again.

As she returned with more game, she was surprised to see the mother doe standing by her fawn.

'So that's that,' thought Nastai with sinking heart. 'She's found her child and will lead it away.'

But the doe remained.

That winter much snow fell. It was hard for the two wild deer to clear the snow and eat the moss. So Nastai fed the doe and the little fawn from her supply of moss and grass. Then, to her delight, the buck and his son appeared, followed by other members of the herd.

The girl sat by her warm hearth, sewing a squirrel coat and foxfur hat with a bird-bone needle, wondering how she was going to keep the herd. When spring came they would surely scatter across the plain. And then once more she harkened to her mother's voice.

Taking careful aim, she loosed her arrows

'Nastai, remember what I taught you.'

Off went Nastai into the forest. She searched long and hard until she found a wolf den with four cubs inside. Fetching the cubs out while the mother was away, she took them home with her.

She fed the cubs on squirrel meat, gave them fresh water to drink, and as they grew she taught them to guard her herd. The cubs obeyed her command, trotted in her steps and were soon as skilled as any dog.

Now she had milk and meat, furs and hides, and plenty of animals for company.

In the meantime, far away, the beggarwoman and her girl were trading away the old man's wealth, while he was hunter, shepherd, cook and cleaner of their house. One year passed, and the fortune was gone. Only the old lame buck remained. So one day, the old woman harnessed it to their rickety sledge and got ready to return.

'We're going back to Saami land,' she said to him. 'You were handy at fishing and hunting there.'

She was also thinking to herself: Yes, and that girl will be long dead by now; the wolves will have left no trace.

So all three drove across plain and hill until they reached the Saami land. As they drew near to the old home they were astonished to see a herd of sturdy reindeer grazing, four well-fed dogs standing guard, and there, alongside the well-kept hut, Nastai sitting in her squirrel coat and foxfur hat.

'Welcome home, Father,' she said joyfully. 'You must be hungry and tired from your journey. Come inside and try some partridge broth, and rest upon my feather bed.'

The old man stared from the herd of reindeer to the old lame buck, from his gentle daughter to the two beggarwomen – and slowly his hand went to his head. Then, for the first time in his life, he opened his mouth and roared like a rutting deer.

'You evil woman, be gone at once. And take your daughter with you!'

With all his strength, he struck the buck upon its rump and off it rushed the way it had come, dragging the two women back to their own land.

And never again did he stray from his daughter's home.

The Nagging Husband

This amusing tale has many versions; this one
comes from Tallin in Estonia

A nagging husband was for ever telling his wife what an easy time she had of it.

'There I am toiling in the fields all day, while you lounge about the house, all snug and warm!' he would say.

As a rule, his wife just sighed, ignoring her husband's taunts; but one day her patience frayed.

'Right!' she said. 'If my job's so easy, let's change places for a day. I'll go to the fields and you can stay at home and mind the house.'

The man smiled. 'Done,' he said, rubbing his hands. 'Tomorrow I'll do the housework and you'll go to mow the grass.'

Early next morning, before leaving home, the wife explained his duties. 'Have a bowl of porridge ready for my lunch, and churn some butter for my rolls. And don't forget to let the cow out to graze.'

The man only laughed. 'I'll manage somehow,' he said.

As the wife went off, he lit his pipe and pondered on the day ahead. He decided to cook the porridge first – what could be simpler? He filled a pot with water and poured in the oats. Then he set to lighting the iron stove. By the time he had a fire burning underneath the pot, his pipe had gone out several times, and he'd had to leave his work to relight it.

At last the porridge began to bubble as he stirred it well; but just then his attention was caught by the mooing of the cow which, in his bother with the oats, had slipped his mind.

'By the time I take the cow to pasture, the porridge's bound to burn,' he reflected. 'I know what: I'll add more water to the pot to give me extra time.'

So off he went to the well for water and came back with a pailful. In his hurry, though, he tipped so much water into the pot that it put out the fire. There was nothing for it but to start again: he raked out the embers, built the fire anew with sticks and straw, and set the now cold porridge on to heat once more.

Meanwhile, the cow was mooing harder than ever. Of course, he knew full well that in taking the cow to graze, the porridge would boil over and douse the fire. What was he to do?

'I know. I'll tether the old cow to a post beside the barn, and she can eat grass there – it's just as sweet as in the meadow.'

So he led the cow out of the barn, hitched a rope from one leg to a doorpost and dashed back to the stove.

As he reached the kitchen, however, he suddenly recalled the butter had to be churned – and off he ran into the barn to fetch the churn and jug of cream.

Still in the best of spirits, he set to churn the cream. It was thirsty work and he had time to spare, so he left off for a moment to quench his thirst from the cider barrel in the barn.

In his haste he forgot to shut the kitchen door.

Oh dear, oh dear!

Just at that moment a sow and her seven piglets were rooting through the yard and, seeing the kitchen open, poked their snouts inside. Spotting the intruders, he quickly ran back to the house, clean forgetting to turn off the cider tap.

Too late! There were the pigs squelching happily in the upset cream, grunting and gobbling to their hearts' content. So angry was he that he snatched up the first thing to hand – a log – and aimed it at the sow. Crack! It hit her smack on the head, killing her outright.

He drove the squealing piglets out of the kitchen, one by one, and finally dragged the dead sow by the tail into the yard.

By now he was red in the face and puffing like a billy goat. Yet he had no time to rest for he suddenly remembered the cider tap. Hurrying back into the barn, he found the place awash with cider and the barrel empty. What a terrible mess!

In desperation he glanced about the barn in search of more cream to make the butter. Luckily, he found another jugful and set to churning it to butter once again. By and by, it occurred to him that the empty cider barrel might well crack if left to dry out. So he dashed back to the well again.

Yet as he ran out of the kitchen, still carrying the churn, he did not see the rope that tied the cow. He tripped and pitched headlong on his face, squelch, into a cowpat. And as the heavy churn flew from his grasp, it landed – crack! – upon the poor cow's leg. She slumped groaning to the ground, her leg broken clean in half.

Wiping his face, he staggered on to the well, dragging the churn behind him; this he now placed on the well ledge as he lowered the pail.

Oh dear me! Can you guess? As he was hauling up the pail, it caught against the churn, knocking it down the well with an enormous splash. What a dreadful to-do!

Now that the cream and churn were in the well he could not make the butter – his wife would have to do without. Gloomily, he turned back to fill the cider barrel with water and as he poured it in, his nose began to twitch. Was something burning?

'Oh darn it!' he muttered crossly. 'That's the porridge; I clean forgot.'

Back in the kitchen he tasted the burnt mess, and thought it might just be eatable if only he could add some butter. So off he trudged to the barn again to see if there might be butter somewhere in a bin.

He searched high and low; it seemed his luck was out. But then, coming to the last bin, he leaned over to take a better look – and toppled in head first!

The flour at the bottom got into his nose and throat, making him sneeze and cough. The more he struggled to get out, the tighter he

The more he struggled to get out, the tighter he became stuck

became stuck, and there he had to stay, kicking his legs up in the air.

When the wife returned from the fields, she was surprised to find no one home. But what a sight met her gaze!

The sow lay on her back – stone dead.

The kitchen floor was awash with cream.

The cow lay beside the barn with a broken leg.

Streams of cider ran through the barn door.

The butter churn had disappeared.

The porridge pot was burned black.

And her husband was nowhere to be seen!

Only when she peered into the barn did she see two legs kicking wildly from a flour bin. At once she pulled him out and helped to dust him down.

She said nothing of the dreadful mess. She just tidied up, cooked some porridge, left some in the pot for him, and went back to the fields.

Thus the day came to a close.

But from that day on the husband never nagged his wife again. Nor did he ever boast that his work was harder than hers.

Gulnara the Tartar Warrior

A Tartar story from the border region of West Siberia and Mongolia

In the blue-topped mountains of Altai, there once lived three girls with their father and a skewbald mare. The land around was ruled by a cruel, wasteful Khan who was for ever waging war, which he paid for by charging his people high taxes.

One day, a rider came to the camp with a message. 'Our Khan is forming an army for war with Khan Kuzlun; you, Olekshin, must come at once.'

The poor old fellow was most upset.

'I'm no good for war,' he said. 'My bones are brittle, my teeth are few, my eyes are dim, my hair's as white as snow.'

But the rider warned, 'If you do not go, they'll come to fetch you.'

As the man rode off, Olekshin wrung his hands and wailed, 'If only I had a son instead of daughters, he'd have gone to war in place of me.'

At that, his eldest daughter, Tazkira, cried. 'Father, you are too old to go to war. Let me take your place.'

So saying, she slung the bow across her back, strapped on the sword and armour, and mounted the skewbald mare. Then, with her black plait streaming in the wind, she rode off to serve the Khan.

On the way she crossed hills and streams and desert plains, until she came to Temir-taiga – the Iron Mountain. And there a black fox with a tail three leagues long barred her way. The skewbald mare took fright, snorted and turned about. No matter how hard the girl pulled on the reins, she could not stop the creature's headlong flight. The mare did not halt until she reached home, throwing Tazkira senseless to the ground.

When she opened her eyes, she saw her father bending over her.

'You have only wasted time,' he grumbled. 'Now I shall be punished by the Khan for being late.'

Old man Olekshin put on his black bow and armour, muttering to himself, 'Daughters are like stones in a mother's belly. Oh for a son!'

Just as he was about to depart, his second daughter, Anara, ran up and firmly seized the reins.

'You are too old for war,' she cried. 'Let me take your place.'

'Then mind you don't turn back,' he said.

She buckled on her father's sword, slung the black bow across her back, mounted the skewbald mare and went on her way.

She crossed hills and streams and desert plains, arriving at last at Temir-taiga. Suddenly, a wolf with a tail three leagues long darted from the dark jaws of the mountain and blocked her way.

The mare reared up in fright, turned about and raced away so fast that the girl was senseless when she reached home.

'You have only wasted time,' her father grumbled when he saw his second daughter. 'I shall be punished by the Khan for being late.'

Bemoaning his fate, old man Olekshin quickly buckled on his sword. But just as he was about to depart, his youngest daughter, Gulnara, came running up, snatched the bridle from his hands and cried, 'Stop, Father, I shall go to the Khan instead of you.'

With that she went to put on the armour; but it was too small. Old man Olekshin had to work all day and night to make the armour fit her, so big and strong was she. At last she was able to put it on, together with sword and bow. Tossing her black plait across one shoulder, she mounted the skewbald mare and raced off like the wind.

Now, that sturdy steed had borne many riders in the past with ease, but soon her back was bent, her hoofs sank down at every step.

All the same, Gulnara drove her over hills and streams and desert plains until they came to Temir-taiga. And there a six-horned stag blocked their path. At once the skewbald mare reared up, snorted with fear and tried to turn about; but the girl pulled tight upon the bit and held her still. Drawing back her black bow she loosed an arrow at the stag, pinning it to the iron wall. Then she lashed her mount hard and galloped on.

On and on she rode until at last she came to the Khan's iron tent. Boldly, she went straight in and sat down between the entrance and the fire.

The Khan glanced up in surprise.

'What lord are you who bows not before the Khan?' he growled.

'I am no lord. I am Gulnara, a simple Tartar maid,' she replied. 'Deep are the years of my father; his bones are brittle, his eyes are dim, his once black hair is now like snow. I come here in his stead.'

'My horde is already halfway to Khan Kuzlun's camp,' the great Khan said. 'How will you overtake it?'

'That is no trial,' she said.

With that she strode from the iron tent, mounted her steed and rushed off like the wind. So fast did she ride that she brushed cobwebs from the sky and kicked up sand so high it dimmed the sun. In no time at all she overtook the Golden Horde and was soon riding alongside the nine generals who were bearing the nine yak-tail standards.

Gulnara was the only girl among the nine thousand warriors of the Khan.

Soon the generals began to moan.

'What use is a girl to us?'

'War is for men.'

'She'll run off home once the fighting starts.'

Gulnara ignored their taunts.

Presently, they came to a dark forest that had no end. The nine generals told their men to cut a pathway through. All that day they laboured without cease, yet when they retired to their tents at dusk,

Gulnara stood upon a mound before them, proud and tall

only a few paces had been cleared, so dense were the trees.

Next dawn, as the first rays of the sun shone down, Gulnara mounted her skewbald mare and galloped off. When she was some way from the horde, she halted, plucked an arrow from her quiver and fitted it to her bow. The two ends of the bow bent together, sparks flew from her thumbs and fire flared upon the arrow head. Off winged the arrow towards the forest. It split the trees in two like the parting of a woman's hair.

When they beheld this wonder, the generals stood amazed. The soldiers began to mutter among themselves.

'This is no girl! No maid could shoot as well as that!'

Angry at their words, Gulnara stood upon a mound before them, proud and tall; then she bared her breasts for all to see – there could be no doubt. An awkward silence fell upon the horde. The once bold soldiers bowed their heads in shame, their loose tongues stilled.

The horde advanced along the pathway of the arrow until they reached a river that was both swift and broad. On the opposite bank were the tents of their enemy, Khan Kuzlun; but there was no way across.

The nine generals called a council. What could they do? There seemed no way on. While the horde slept that night, however, Gulnara rose and changed herself into a bird. She fluttered across the raging waters and landed beside the smoke hole of Kuzlun's tent. And there she sat, listening to the talk.

Old Kuzlun was sitting by the fire speaking to his wife.

'The horde will never cross the river; we are safe,' he said.

'Is there really no way across?' she asked.

'There is, but only I know where,' Kuzlun replied. 'It is by Temir-terek, the Iron Poplar Tree.'

'But what if the horde find it?'

'Then I should turn my herds and followers into ashes and grains of sand, leaving behind just the old and lame,' he said.

'And what of us?'

'I would turn myself into a camel, you into an iron last and our daughter, Altyn-yustook, into a silver birch.'

Having heard this talk, Gulnara flew back across the river and slept till dawn.

As the sun's first rays shone down, Gulnara called to the sleeping men, 'Come, wake up and follow me.'

She mounted her skewbald mare and rode to Temir-terek, found the crossing – a horsehair bridge strung between the banks – and led the way across.

But when they reached the enemy camp, there was nothing to be seen: no Kuzlun Khan, no wife, no herds, no followers. Only the old and lame lay in their tents.

'We shall have to tell the Khan that we slew Kuzlun and took just these few prisoner,' the generals said.

Meanwhile, Gulnara was tying an old camel to the tail of her skewbald mare.

'What do you need that camel for?' they asked.

'To help my father carry wood,' she said.

Then she began to scrape up sand and ash to fill her pouch.

'Why do you want the sand and ash?' they asked.

'My father can use the ash when he forges tools,' she said. 'And he can sprinkle sand upon the hot iron.'

With that she picked up an iron last that lay beside the tent.

'Don't you have iron at home to make a last?' they asked.

'Why make a last when here's one already made? It will serve my sister for softening hides.'

Finally, she set to pulling up a silver birch; as they looked on in surprise, the generals cried, 'As if we don't have birch trees in our land! What is that for?'

'To make a handle for a broom,' was all she said.

The horde started on its homeward march and came in time to the Khan. Presenting the old and the lame prisoners to him, the generals declared, 'We had a terrible battle with Khan Kuzlun, but through our skill and cunning we overcame him, killing all his men. These few are all that are left alive.'

'A pity you did not take Kuzlun alive,' sighed the Khan.

At this Gulnara laughed loudly, and all eyes turned her way.

'Now see my trophies,' she declared.

As she led the camel forward, she struck it hard – and there, cowering on the ground, was Kuzlun himself.

Then she threw the iron last upon the earth and it turned into the wife of Khan Kuzlun; and when she shook the silver birch, there appeared Altyn-yustook, their daughter.

As the nine generals stared, she took her saddlebags and shook out the sand and ash upon the open plain. At once there sprang up more herds than one could count, more people than the forest trees.

'That is what I have brought,' Gulnara said.

With that she leapt upon her mare and rode off home.

Some say, however, that the story did not end there. They say the nine generals and the Khan plotted to rid themselves of the warrior maid, and invited her back to take her reward.

But inside the iron tent they had prepared a white satin cushion for her to sit upon, and below it was a deep pit full of snakes!

Gulnara was wise as well as strong, and noticed as she came in that they all looked towards the satin seat.

'This cushion is fit only for the Khan,' she cried.

At that the Khan took fright and edged away, his nine generals behind him. But Gulnara seized the Khan in her strong arms, picked him up and set him down on the white satin seat.

The cushion and the Khan plunged below into the pit of snakes.

Then, one by one, she picked up the generals and pitched them down as well. With her own bare hands, she tore the iron tent into little strips until not a scrap remained.

And, mounting her skewbald mare, she rode off home.

'My dear sisters and brothers,' she told the people on her return, 'you may now live in peace. There is no Khan to make you go to war or pay taxes. I shall protect you.'

How proud and happy the people were that their own Gulnara was wiser and stronger than all the generals of the Golden Horde.

Caterina the Wise

A story from Sicily in the south of Italy

Once upon a time there was a clever young woman who lived in Palermo with her father, a rich merchant. She was so wise that she decided every matter in the household. When it came to studying foreign languages or any books, there was none to match her. Recognizing his daughter's talent, her father called her Caterina la Sapiente – Caterina the Wise.

One day, when the girl was sixteen, her mother died. Caterina was so distressed that she shut herself up in her room and would not come out. There she ate and there she slept; she would not think of books or entertainment of any sort.

In despair her father finally summoned a council to discuss what could be done.

'My lords,' he said, 'you know well I have a daughter who is the apple of my eye. Ever since her mother died she has shut herself up in her room and won't even stick her nose outside. What am I to do?'

The council debated for long hours and eventually made its reply: 'Your daughter is famous the world over for her wisdom. Open a school for her, so that she can teach others. That is bound to cure her of her grief.'

Caterina agreed to her father's plan. She hired teachers and hung a sign outside the house:

WHOEVER WISHES TO STUDY
WITH CATERINA THE WISE
IS WELCOME
FREE OF CHARGE

Crowds of children came willingly, and Caterina seated them side by side without distinction.

'But that boy there's a chimney sweep!' someone complained.

'So?' replied Caterina. 'The chimney sweep *should* sit beside the daughter of the king. That way they'll learn better together.'

And school began. Rich or poor, Caterina treated everyone the same. She kept a leather strap in her desk and woe betide anyone who did not work hard!

The reputation of the school so grew that finally the Prince himself decided to attend. So, attired in his royal robes, he came to school and Caterina seated him at the back. When his turn came to do his sums, he got them all wrong and received a hard slap from Caterina that made his ear sting.

Red with shame, the Prince could not wait to get home. Running back to the palace after school, an idea came to him. He immediately sought out his father and made a strange request.

'A favour, Majesty. I wish to marry my teacher Caterina the Wise.'

The King sent forthwith for Caterina's father, who came at once and went down on his knees before the royal throne.

'Arise,' said the king. 'My son has taken a fancy to your daughter. What's to be done? Marry them, I suppose.'

'With pleasure, Majesty,' said the man. 'But I am but a merchant and your son has royal blood.'

'It can't be helped – my son must have his wish,' replied the King.

On returning home, the merchant told his daughter, 'Caterina, the Prince wants to marry you. What do you say?'

'All right,' she said, for she did not really care one way or the other.

Wool for mattresses was not wanting, nor wood for furniture. In a week all was ready for the royal home. The Prince arrived at church with a dozen bridesmaids and the wedding was performed. Once he was alone at home with his bride, however, the Prince said, 'Caterina, do you recall the slap you gave me on my ear? I expect you are sorry now?'

'Sorry? I'll give you another, if you like, on the other ear!'

'You mean you aren't sorry at all?'

'Not the slightest.'

'Right, now I'll teach you a thing or two, and make you beg for mercy,' he cried angrily. Then he called the guard.

'Now, Caterina, this is your last chance. Say you're sorry, or I'll have the guard tie you up and put you in a dungeon.'

'It'll be cooler there,' she said.

So the guard tied a rope around her and lowered her through a trapdoor into a dungeon below; all she had was a little table, a stool, a jug of water and a crust of bread.

Next morning, the Prince opened the trapdoor and called down to his bride, 'Well, how have you spent the night?'

'Most refreshing,' she replied.

'Are you thinking of the slap you gave me?'

'I'm thinking of the one I owe you now,' she said.

Two days passed and hunger forced her to think up a plan. Drawing a steel stay out of her corset, she set to making a hole in the wall. She scraped away until, some time later, she saw a ray of light. Making the hole bigger, she peered through it into the street beyond. And who should be passing by but her father's clerk.

'Don Tommaso! Don Tommaso!' she shouted.

At first Don Tommaso could not understand how the voice was coming from the wall.

'It's me, Caterina. Tell my father I must speak to him at once!'

In no time at all Don Tommaso returned with the merchant and showed him the talking wall.

'Father mine,' she said, 'I'm trapped in a dungeon below the palace. Have a tunnel made from our house to here, with an arch and torch every twenty paces. Leave the rest to me.'

The merchant agreed and in the meantime he brought her food to eat. Roast chicken, hot pies and cakes were passed through the opening.

Three times each day the Prince opened the trapdoor to call down, 'Caterina, are you sorry yet for slapping me?'

'Sorry for what? Just you wait until I get my hands on you – I'll give you something to shout about!'

Finally the tunnel was dug, with an arch and lantern every twenty paces. Caterina could now pass to and fro whenever she wanted.

It was not long before the Prince grew tired of the game. So he opened the trapdoor one day and called down, 'Caterina, I am going to Naples. Have you anything to say?'

'Have a good time, and write to me the moment you arrive.'

'Do you think I should go?'

'What? Are you still here? I thought you'd gone.'

So he left.

No sooner had he gone than Caterina hurried off to her father's house.

'Papa, now is the time to help. Have a ship ready for me to sail at once, with servants, fine dresses and a governess. I'm going to Naples. Once there I'll rent a mansion opposite the palace.'

Off sailed the ship with Caterina on board, just ahead of the Prince's brigantine.

In Naples, Caterina would appear each day upon the balcony of her mansion in a gown more glittering than the one before. And each day the Prince would see her and sigh, 'How like my Caterina that lady is!'

He fell so much in love that finally he sent a messenger, asking if he might visit her.

'By all means,' she replied.

The Prince arrived in grand attire and made a great fuss of her before sitting down to talk.

'Tell me, Signora,' he said, 'are you married?'

'Are you?' she replied.

'Oh no,' he said quickly.

Caterina would appear each day upon the balcony

'Then nor am I.'

'But you are so much like a lady who took my fancy in Palermo. I wonder: would you consent to be my wife?'

'With pleasure,' she replied.

Within eight days they were wed.

At the end of nine months Caterina gave birth to a baby boy fairer than words can tell.

'Princess,' said the Prince, 'what name shall we give our son?'

'Naples,' she said.

So they named him Naples.

Two years passed, and the Prince decided to go on his travels once again. Of course, the Princess was unhappy at being left alone with her young son, and she told him so. But all the Prince would do was sign a paper declaring that the boy was his first-born and would one day be king. Then he left for Genoa.

No sooner had he departed than Caterina hired a ship to take her to Genoa with servants, governess and all the rest. Since the ship was smaller than the Prince's, it reached Genoa first. At once she rented a mansion opposite the palace, so that when the Prince arrived he saw her on the balcony.

'*Santo cielo!*' he exclaimed. 'How like Caterina the Wise she is, not to mention the lady of Naples!'

And he sent a messenger, asking her to receive a visit from him. Caterina gave her consent, and soon afterwards he arrived at her mansion. After praising this and that, he asked directly, 'Are you married, Signora?'

'Are you?' she replied.

'A widower, with one son.'

'Then I'm a widow too.'

'It is uncanny,' said the Prince. 'You so resemble a lady I once knew in Palermo, and another in Naples.'

'We all have seven doubles in the world, so people say,' she said.

They were married within the week. Nine months later Caterina had another son, even fairer than the first. The Prince was overjoyed.

'What shall we call him?' he asked his wife.

'Genoa,' Caterina said.

So they baptized him Genoa.

Two years passed, and the Prince grew restless once again.

'Are you abandoning your son and me?' Caterina asked.

'Well, I'll sign a paper so that people know the boy is my son and heir.'

While he was making arrangements to depart for Venice, Caterina hired another ship to sail there too, with servants, governess, finery and new clothes. And off she sailed in the wake of the Prince; her swift vessel arrived in Venice before the Prince's ship.

'*Mama mia!*' exclaimed the Prince when he arrived in Venice and saw the woman upon her balcony opposite. 'She is the image of my wife in Genoa, who is the image of my wife in Naples, who is so like Caterina the Wise! How can it be? Caterina is in a Palermo dungeon; the Neapolitan woman is in Naples; the Genoese in Genoa; while this Venetian is here in Venice!'

Puzzled, he sent a messenger and soon followed with a visit.

'I must tell you, Signora, that you are so like several other ladies I used to know.'

'Indeed,' said Caterina. 'People say we have seven doubles about the world.'

So the usual talk went on its way.

'Are you married?'

'Are you?'

'No, I'm a widower with two sons.'

'Then I'm a widow.'

Within the week they were wed. This time Caterina had a daughter, as radiant as the sun and moon.

'What shall we call her?' asked the Prince.

'Venice,' Caterina said.

And Venice she became.

Another two years went by. Then one day the Prince announced he was going to Palermo, alone. But before he went, since he was an honourable man, he drew up a document declaring that Venice was indeed his daughter, the royal princess.

Off he sailed, but Caterina reached Palermo first. She went straight to her father's house, walked through the tunnel and back to her dungeon. As soon as the Prince arrived at the palace, he ran to his room, pulled up the trapdoor and shouted down, 'How are you, Caterina?'

'Just fine,' she replied coolly.

'Are you sorry now for the slap you gave me?'

'Have you been thinking,' said Caterina, 'of the slap I owe you?'

'If you don't say sorry I'll take another wife.'

'Go on then. I won't stop you.'

'Say you're sorry and I'll take you back,' he said one last time.

'No.'

So the Prince made it known he was seeking a new wife. He wrote to all the queens and kings for portraits of their daughters, so that he could choose the best. The pictures duly arrived and the one that took his fancy was of a princess of England. In no time at all the entire royal family of England arrived in Palermo, and the wedding was set for the following day.

And what do you think Caterina the Wise did?

She had three grand suits made for her children – Naples, Genoa and Venice; and she dressed herself as the Princess she truly was, and went to the palace with her children.

Just as the wedding procession was approaching, she said loudly to her children, 'Prince Naples, Princess Venice, Prince Genoa, go and kiss your father's hand.'

And the children ran forward to kiss the Prince's hand.

At the sight of his children, he fell on his knees and wept.

The English princess turned her back and stalked off angrily, returning forthwith to England.

In the meantime, Caterina explained the mystery of the ladies who looked alike. And never again did the Prince leave home, nor cease to be sorry for what he had done.

Together they reopened Caterina's school and once again children came from all over Italy to learn from Caterina the Wise. (Though the Prince never did manage to learn his sums!)

Oona and
the Giant Cuchulain

A tall tale from Ireland

Of all the giants that ever walked the vales of Ireland, the giant Cuchulain was the strongest. With a blow of his mighty fist he could squash a mountain into a cowpat, and he went about the land with one such cowpat in his pocket to scare the other giants.

He scared them all right. They tried to keep out of his way, but he hunted them down, one by one, and beat the living daylights out of them; then they scampered off into the mountains to lick their wounds.

There was one giant, though, that Cuchulain had not yet thrashed, and that was Finn Mac Cool. The reason was simple: Finn Mac Cool was so afraid of Cuchulain that he kept well out of his way. He even built his house atop a windy mountain to keep a lookout all about him; and whenever the mighty giant appeared in the distance, Finn was off like a shot from a cannon, hiding in bush or bog or barrow.

But Finn could not keep his foe at bay for ever. And Cuchulain had vowed he would not rest until he had flattened the cowardly Finn. Finn knew the day must come. Do you know how? By sucking his thumb: that made all things clear to him.

So there he was, this Finn, sitting outside his house upon the windy mountain, sucking his great thumb. And, oh dear me! rushing indoors shivering like a jelly, he cried to his wife Oona, 'Cuchulain is coming this way. And this time there's no escape; my thumb tells me so!'

'What time is he due?' asks Oona.

Finn sucked his thumb again. 'At three o'clock this afternoon. And do you know what he means to do? Squash me flat and carry me in his pocket along with his cowpat!'

'Now, now, Finn,' says Oona, 'just leave this to me. Haven't I pulled you from the mire many times before?'

'Indeed you have,' said Finn. And he stopped his shivering.

In the meantime Oona went down to three friends at the foot of the mountain, and at each house she borrowed an iron griddle. Once home with her three griddles, she baked half a dozen cakes, each as big as a basket; and inside three she put an iron griddle while the dough was soft. Then she placed the cakes in a row upon two shelves: three above, three below, so that she would know which one was which.

At two o'clock she glanced out of the window and spied a speck on the horizon; she guessed it was Cuchulain coming. Straightaway she dressed Finn in nightgown and frilly night cap, and tucked him into a big wicker cradle.

'Now, Finn,' she says, 'you'll be your own baby. Lie still and leave all to me. Suck your thumb so as you'll know what I want you to do.'

Finn did as he was told.

'Oh, and by the way,' she says, 'where does that bully of a giant keep all his strength?'

Finn stuck his thumb in his mouth, then said, 'His strength is in the middle finger of his right hand. Without that finger he'd be as weak as a baby.'

With that they sat waiting for himself to come. And it was not long before a giant fist pounded on the door.

Finn screwed his eyes shut, drew the blanket up round his nose, and tried to keep his teeth from chattering. Boldly Oona flung open the door – and there stood the mighty Cuchulain.

'Is this the house of Finn Mac Cool?' asks he.

'It is indeed,' says Oona. 'Come in and sit you down.'

Cuchulain took a seat and stared about him.

'That's a fine-looking baby you have there, Mrs Mac Cool,' says he. 'Would his father be at home? I wonder.'

'Faith, he's not,' says she. 'He went tearing down the mountain a few hours ago, said he was out to catch some pipsqueak called Cuchulain. Heaven help the poor man when my Finn lays hands on him; there won't be a hair or toenail of him left.'

'I am Cuchulain himself, Mrs Mac Cool,' says the visitor. 'And I've been on your husband's track this past year or more. Yet he's always hiding from me; for sure he can't be so very big and strong?'

'*You* are Cuchulain!' says Oona, scornful-like. 'Did you ever see my Finn?'

'Well, no. How could I? He always gives me the slip.'

'Gives you the slip, begorrah!' says she. 'Gives you the thrashing of your life, more likely. I mean you no ill, Sir, but if you take my advice you'll steer clear of him. He's as hard as rock and swift as the wind. Which reminds me: would you do me a favour and turn the house round, the wind is on the turn.'

'*Turn the house round?*' stammered Cuchulain. 'Did my ears hear right?'

'For sure,' says Oona. 'That's what Finn does when the wind's in the east.'

Cuchulain stood up and went outside. He crooked the middle finger of his right hand three times, seized the house in his arms and turned it back to front.

When Finn felt the house turn, he pulled the blanket over his head and his teeth chattered all the more.

But Oona just nodded her thanks as if it was quite natural, then asked another favour.

'With all this dry weather we're having,' says she, 'I'm clean out of water. Can you fill this jug for me?'

'And where will I fill it?' asks Cuchulain.

'Do you see that big rock on top of yonder hill? When we need water Finn lifts that rock and takes water from the spring underneath. Just as soon as you fetch some water I'll put the kettle on and make you a nice cup of tea. You'll need a cup or two if you're to escape the clutches of the mighty Finn.'

With a frown, Cuchulain took the jug and walked down the mountain and up yonder hill. When he arrived at the rock, he stood and scratched his head in wonder: it was at least as tall as himself, and twice as wide. He held up his right hand, crooked the middle finger nine times, then took the rock in both brawny arms and heaved. With a mighty effort, he tore the rock out of the ground, and four hundred feet of solid rock below as well. And out gushed a stream that gurgled and roared down the hillside so loudly it made Finn shut his ears with both hands.

'Dear wife,' he cried, 'if that giant lays his hands on me, he'll crush every bone in my body.'

'Wisht, man!' says Oona, 'he has to find you first.'

And she greeted the jug-bearer with a smile of thanks as he came through the door.

'Thank you kindly,' says she. 'Now take a seat while I put the kettle on.'

As soon as the kettle had boiled and the tea was poured, Oona set three cakes before Cuchulain – those with the iron griddles in.

All that work had made Cuchulain hungry. Smacking his lips, he picked up a cake and took a great bite of it. Oh musha! With a wild yell he spat out the cake and his two front teeth as well.

'What cake is this! It's as hard as nails.'

'That's Finn's favourite cake,' says Oona. 'He's mighty partial to it; so is the baby in the cradle. Perhaps it's too hard-baked for a weakling like you. Here, try this one, it's a mite softer than the first.'

It certainly smelt appetizing. This time he took an even bigger bite. But, oh musha! Again he spat it out along with two more giant teeth.

'You can keep your cakes,' he shouted, 'or I'll have no teeth left.'

'God bless us!' exclaims Oona. 'There's no call to shout so loud

Cuchulain took the jug and walked down the mountain

and wake the baby up. It's not my fault your jaws are weak.'

Now, just at that moment Finn sucked his thumb and guessed at once what Oona wanted him to do. Opening his mouth he let out the greatest, rip-roaring yell he'd ever made.

'Yoowwwlllllllllllllllllll . . .'

'Well, I be jiggered,' spluttered Cuchulain, his hair standing on end. 'What a pair of tonsils that baby's got! Does it take after its father?'

'When his father gives a shout,' says Oona, 'you can hear him from here to Timbuctoo!'

Cuchulain began to feel uneasy. Perhaps he was wrong to come in search of Finn Mac Cool. Glancing nervously towards the cradle, he saw the child was sucking its thumb again.

'He'll be crying for some cake any minute now,' says Oona. 'It's his feeding time.'

Just then, Finn began to howl, 'CAAA-AAKKE!'

'Put that in your mouth,' says she. And she handed Finn a cake from the top shelf.

'How can a baby eat that?' said Cuchulain scornfully.

But in the twinkling of an eye, Finn had eaten every crumb, then roared out again, 'CAAA-AAKKE!'

When the baby was well into his third cake, Cuchulain got up to go.

'I'm off now, Mrs Mac Cool,' he says. 'If that baby's anything like its dad, Finn'll be more than a match for me. 'Tis a bonny baby you have, ma'am.'

'If you're so fond of babies, come and have a closer look at this one,' says she.

And she took Cuchulain by the arm to guide him to the cradle, removing the blanket from Finn as she did so. Thereupon Finn kicked his legs in the air and yelled at the top of his voice.

'By golly, what a pair of legs he has on him!' gasped Cuchulain.

'You ought to have seen his father at that age,' says Oona. 'Why, he was out in the bogs wrestling with bulls at one year old.'

'Is that a fact?' sighed Cuchulain, eager to get away from the house before Finn returned.

'The baby's teeth are coming through well, though,' continues Oona. 'Have a feel of them.'

Thinking to please the woman before making his escape, Cuchulain put his fingers into the baby's mouth to feel its teeth.

And can you guess what happened?

When he pulled his fingers out, there were only four left: his middle finger had been bitten off.

You could have heard the yell from there to Venezuela!

Now that his strength was gone, the once mighty Cuchulain began to grow smaller and smaller, until he was no bigger than the cake he had bitten into. High above him Oona and Finn Mac Cool laughed and mocked the little man. The tiny figure tottered out of the house and down the mountain, fleeing for his life. And he was never seen again in Ireland.

As for Finn, he was ever grateful for the brains of his dear wife Oona.

Aina-kizz and
the Black-Bearded Bai

A story of how a young girl outwits a rich man –
or bai – from Soviet Central Asia

There was once a young girl who lived with her father, a
woodcutter. Their home was a tumbledown shack and a gap-
toothed axe was the only tool they owned. A lame old horse and mule
were their transport.

But, as wise folk say, a rich family's fortune is in its herds, a poor
family's in its children.

And true enough, whenever the old woodcutter gazed upon his
daughter, who was only nine, he forgot all his cares and woes. The
girl's name was Aina-kizz and she was so clever that people came
from miles around to ask her advice.

One day the woodcutter loaded his horse with a pile of logs and
told the girl, 'I am going to market and will be home by dusk. If I sell
my logs I'll bring you a little present.'

'May good luck be with you, Father,' she replied. 'But do be
careful, for one man's gain at market is another's loss.'

The woodcutter went on his way, arriving in time at the bazaar; he
stood to one side beside his horse and awaited buyers for his wood.
But no one came. As it was getting late, a rich bai came strutting

through the market, showing off his silk robe and stroking his black beard. Catching sight of the poor man and his wood-laden horse, he called, 'Hey, old fellow, what will you take for your logs?'

'A single tanga, sir.'

'Will you sell your wood exactly as it is?' the bai asked with a sly grin.

The woodman nodded slowly, unsure of what he meant.

'Here's your coin,' said the bai. 'Bring your horse and follow me.'

When they came to the bai's big house, the poor man went to unpack the logs from the horse's back. But the bai shouted in his ear, 'Stop! I bought the wood "exactly as it is" – which means the horse belongs to me since it's carrying the wood. If you're not content, we'll go before the judge.'

As wise folk say: just as a bad master can turn a steed into a useless nag, so a bad judge can turn right to wrong. And so it was.

Having heard the two complaints, the judged stroked his beard, glanced at the bai's silk robe and gave his verdict: the woodman had got his just desserts. It served him right for agreeing to the terms!

The rich man laughed in the woodman's face; and he, poor man, trudged wearily home to tell his tale to Aina-kizz.

'Never mind, Father, tomorrow I'll go to market,' she said. 'Who knows, I may be luckier than you.'

Next day at dawn, she loaded up the mule with logs and, driving it along with her switch, made her way to the bazaar. There she stood beside the mule until the selfsame bai approached her.

'Hey, girl, what will you take for your wood?' he called.

'Two tangas.'

'And will you trade it exactly as it is?' he said.

'Certainly,' she replied, 'if you pay the money exactly as it is.'

'Surely, surely,' said the bai, holding out his hand to show her two gold coins. 'Follow me.'

The same thing happened to her as to her father. But she did not mind. As the bai smilingly paid her two coins, she stood her ground.

'Sir,' she said, 'you bought my wood just as it is and you have my mule together with the wood. But you gave your word to pay the price exactly as it is. So now I want your arm as well.'

The bai was taken aback. His beard shook with rage as he cursed her soundly; but she did not yield at all. At last, they set off together to the judge. That worthy man heard the complaint, yet this time he could not help the bai: he had to pay two tangas for the wood and another fifty for his arm.

How the rich man regretted that he had bought the wood, the horse and the mule. Handing over the money before the judge, he told the girl, 'You outwitted me this time, but a sparrow cannot match a hawk. I bet you cannot tell a bigger lie than I can; I'll put five hundred on it. You put the fifty I paid you and whichever lie the judge says is the bigger wins the bet. What do you say?'

'Done,' said Aina-kizz.

Winking to the judge, the rich bai began his tale.

'One day, before I was born, I found three ears of corn in my pocket and tossed them through the window. Next morning my yard had become a field of corn so thick and tall it took riders ten days to find a way through. And then, by the by, forty of my best goats were lost in the corn. No matter how hard I searched, I could not find them. They had vanished without a trace.

'In late summer, when the corn was ripe, my labourers gathered the harvest in and the flour was ground. Rolls were baked and I ate one, all fresh and hot. And what do you think? Out of my mouth leaped one goat, followed by a second and a third ... Then, one by one, out came all forty beasts, bleating hard. How fat they had become – each one bigger than a four-year bull!'

When the bai fell silent, even the judge sat open-mouthed. But Aina-kizz did not turn a hair.

'Sir,' she said, 'with such wise men as you, lies can be truly grand. Pray, listen now to my humble tale.' And she told her story.

'Once I planted a cotton seed in my garden. And, do you know, next day a cotton bush had grown right up to the clouds; it cast a shadow as far as three days' journey across the sands. When the cotton was ripe, I picked and cleaned it, and sold it at market. With the money I received I bought forty fine camels, loaded them with

The smiles upon the two men's faces quickly dimmed

silks and bade my brother take the caravan to Samarkand.

'Off he went dressed in his best silk robe; but I had no news from him for three whole years. Only the other day did I hear he had been robbed and slain by a black-bearded bai. I gave up all hope of finding the villain, yet now, by chance, I have discovered him.

'It is you, bai, for you are wearing my brother's best silk robe!'

At these words, the smiles upon the two men's faces quickly dimmed. What was the judge to do? If he said the story was a whopping lie, the bai would lose five hundred gold coins; that was the bet. Yet if he said she spoke the truth ... that was even worse. She would claim compensation for her brother and, besides, for forty fine camels loaded with rich silks.

The bai roared like a wounded bull, 'You lie, you lie! That's the biggest lie I've ever heard! Take your five hundred tangas, take my silk robe, only go and leave me in peace.'

With a smile, Aina-kizz counted out the coins, wrapped them in the robe and walked back home.

Fearing for his daughter, the woodcutter was waiting anxiously at the door to greet her. How he hugged her to him, not even remarking on the missing mule.

'Father, I sold our mule with all the logs, exactly as it was.'

'Oh, my poor child,' he muttered, 'so that hard-hearted bai has swindled you as well.'

'But I received a fair price for the wood,' she said quietly. And she handed him the silken robe.

'This is a handsome robe,' he said sadly. 'But what good is it to me? Without our horse and mule, we shall likely starve to death.'

Thereupon, Aina-kizz unrolled the robe before her father's astonished gaze and the golden coins showered upon the floor. Then she told him the tale of her adventures in the town.

How he laughed and cried in turn, listening to her tale. She ended the story thus: 'Father, where the rich keep their fortune, so the poor keep their cunning. A girl's wise head is better than a man's full purse.'

A Pottle o' Brains

An old tale from Lincolnshire in England

Once in these parts, and not so long ago, there lived a wise old dame. Some said she was a fairy, but they said it in a whisper, in case she should overhear and do them mischief.

If you were ill, she could tell you how to cure yourself with herbs; and she could mix possets that would drive out pain in a twinkling. She could advise you what to do if your cows took sick or if you had toothache; and she could tell the lads and lasses if their sweethearts were untrue.

One day, as she sat at her door peeling potatoes, over the stile and up the path came a tall lad with big ears and goggle eyes, hands in pockets.

'That's a fool, if ever was,' said the wise old dame, nodding her head. And she threw some potato peel over her left shoulder for luck.

'Evenin', missis,' says he, ' 'tis a fine night for it.'

'Aye,' says she, and went on peeling.

'It'll maybe rain,' says he, shifting from right foot to left.

'Maybe,' says she.

'And maybe it won't,' says he, looking at the sky.

'Maybe not,' says she.

He took off his hat and scratched his head.

'Well,' says he, 'that's the weather done, now let me see ... The crops are doing fine.'

'Fine,' says she.

'And the pigs are fattening,' says he.

'They are that,' says she.

'And, and . . .' says he, coming to a halt. 'I reckon I'll get down to business now: have you any brains to sell?'

'That depends,' says she. 'If you want king's brains, priest's brains, judge's brains, I don't stock them.'

'Oh, no,' says he, 'just an ordinary pottle o' brains, same as folk about here have, something common-like.'

'Well, then,' says the woman, 'I might manage that if you can help yourself.'

'How's that, missis?' says he.

'Just so,' says she, eyeing her potatoes. 'Bring me the heart of the thing you like the best, and I'll tell you where to get your brains.'

He scratched his head. 'How can I do that?' he says.

'That's not for me to say,' says she. 'Find out for yourself, lad, unless you wish to be stupid all your days. And you must also answer me a riddle, so I can see you have your wits about you. Now, good evening.' And she took her pile of potatoes indoors.

So off went the fool to his mother and told her of the wise woman's words.

'I reckon I'll have to kill our pig,' says he, 'for I like pork scratchings best of all.'

'Then do it, lad,' his mother says. 'For certain, 'twill be a good thing for you if you can look after yourself.'

So he kills his pig, and next day goes off to the wise woman's place. And there she sat, reading a great book.

'Evenin', missis,' says he, 'I've brought you the heart of the thing I like the best. I'll leave it on the table all wrapped up.'

'Aye so,' says she, peering at him over her spectacles. 'Here's your riddle then: What runs without feet?'

He took off his hat and scratched his head; he thought and thought but could not tell.

'Go on your way,' says she, 'for you've not brought the right thing

---

yet. I've no brains for you today.'

With that she clapped the book together and turned her back.

So he went back down the path and over the stile and sat down by the roadside to cry. And how he cried. By and by, up came a lass who lived nearby.

'What's up, lad? Can I help?'

'Oooo, I've killed my pig, but cannot gain a pottle o' brains,' wails he.

'What are you talking about?'

And down she sits beside him to hear about the wise woman and the pig. He says, besides, he has no one to look after him.

'Well,' says she, 'I wouldn't mind living with you myself.'

'Could you do it?' says he, surprised.

'Oh, I dare say,' says she. 'Folk say that fools make decent husbands. I reckon I might have you. Can you cook?'

'Aye, I can,' says he.

'And scrub?'

'Surely.'

'And mend my clouts?'

'I can that,' says he.

'Then I reckon you'll do as well as anybody,' says she.

'That's settled then,' says he. 'I'll come and fetch you when I've told my Ma.'

He gave her his lucky penny and went off home.

When he got home and told his mother he wished to marry, the poor woman was very cross.

'What!' says she. '*That* lass? No, and that you'll not. She does men's work in the fields and never keeps a clean and tidy house. And there's talk about her in the neighbourhood.'

'But I gave her my lucky penny,' he says.

'Then you're a bigger fool than ever,' says his mother.

Those were the last words the poor woman spoke. For she was so upset that she lay right down and died.

So down sat the fool and the more he thought about it the worse he felt. He remembered how she had nursed him when he was a little lad, and helped him with his sums; and how she had cooked his dinners, and mended his shirts, and put up with his foolish ways; and he felt sorrier and sorrier and began to sob.

'Oh, Ma, Ma,' wails he, 'I liked you best of all.'

As he said that, he thought of the wise dame's words.

'Hout-tout!' says he. 'Must I take her my Ma's heart?'

He thought and thought and scratched his head; then an idea came to him. He took a sack and pushed his mother in. Then he hoisted her on his shoulder and carried her up to the old dame's place.

'Evenin', missis,' says he. 'I reckon I've fetched the right thing this time.' And he plumped the sack down upon the table.

'Maybe,' says she. 'But tell me this: What's yellow and shining, yet isn't gold?'

He scratched his head, but could not tell.

'You've not found the right thing yet, my lad,' says she. 'You're a bigger fool than I thought.' And she shut the door, bang, right in his face.

Feeling sad, off he went to the lass he had met and got himself married to her. He kept the house clean and neat, and cooked her fine dinners; and she worked hard in the fields all day. It pleased them both.

One night he says to her, 'Lass, I'm thinking I like you best of all.'

'That's good to hear,' says she. 'And what then?'

'Should I kill you, do you think, and take your heart up to the wise dame for that pottle o' brains?'

'Lawks, no!' says she, getting scared. 'See here, just you take me to her as I am, heart and all, and I'll help you solve those riddles.'

'Will you so?' says he, doubtful-like. 'I reckon they're too hard for womenfolk.'

'Well,' says she, 'just test me now.'

'What runs without feet?' says he.

'Why, water, of course!' says she.

'Aye, so it does,' says he, scratching his head.

'And what's yellow and shining, yet isn't gold?' says he.

———

'I reckon I've fetched the right thing this time'

'Why, the sun, of course!' says she.

'Faith, so it is,' says he. 'Come, we'll go to the dame at once.'

And off they went. As they came up the path and over the stile, she was sitting at the door, twining straws.

'Evenin', missis,' says he.

'Evenin', Fool,' says she.

'I reckon I've fetched you the right thing at last.'

The wise woman looked at them both and wiped her spectacles.

'Answer my riddles then,' she says. 'What has first no legs, then two legs, then four legs?'

The fool scratched his head, thought and thought, but could not tell.

So the lass whispered in his ear, 'A tadpole.'

'Happen it's a tadpole, missis,' says he at last.

The old dame nodded. 'Now what about the other riddles?'

At once he told her what his wife had said: water and the sun.

The wise woman smiled. 'You've got your pottle o' brains at last,' says she.

'Where are they?' says he, looking about and feeling his head.

'In your wife's head,' says she. 'The only cure for a fool is a good wife. Good evenin' to you!'

The fool and his wife walked home together, quite content. And he never wished for brains again, for his wife had enough for two.

The Maid Who Chose a Husband

A tale from Ghana in West Africa

The maid of Kyerefaso, the Queen Mother's daughter, was as nimble as a deer and wise as an owl. Foruwa, such was she, with head held high, eyes soft and wide with wonder. And she was light of foot, light in all her movements.

As she stepped along the water path like a young deer that had strayed from the thicket, as she sprang along the water path, she was a picture to give the eye a feast. And nobody passed her by but turned to look at her again.

Those of her village said that her voice was like the murmur of a river quietly flowing beneath the shadows of bamboo leaves. They said her smile blossomed like a lily on her lips and rose like the sun.

Butterflies do not fly away from flowers; and Foruwa was the flower of the village. So all the village butterflies tried to draw near her at every turn, crossed and criss-crossed her path. Men said of her, 'She shall be my wife, and mine, and mine, and mine.'

But suns rose and set, moons waxed and waned, and as the days passed Foruwa became no man's wife. She smiled at the butterflies and waved her hand lightly to greet them as she went swiftly about her work, saying, 'Morning, Kweku. Morning, Kwesi. Morning,

As the days passed Foruwa became no man's wife

Kwodo.' That was all.

So they said, even while their hearts thumped for her, 'Proud! Foruwa is too proud.'

When they came together, the men would say, 'There goes a silly girl. She is not just stiff-in-the-neck proud, not just breasts-stuck-out-I-am-the-only-girl-in-the-village proud. What kind of pride is that?'

The end of the year came round again, bringing the season of festivals. For the gathering-in of corn, yams and cocoa there were harvest celebrations. And there were bride-meetings too.

The Queen Mother was there, tall and wise, standing before the men, and there was silence.

'What news, what news do you bring?' she asked.

'We come with dusty brows from our path-finding, Mother. We come with weary thorn-pricked feet. We come to bathe in the coolness of your peaceful stream. We come to offer our manliness to create new life.'

'It is well. Come, maidens, women all, join the men in dance, for they offer themselves to create new life.'

Yet there was one girl who did not dance.

'What, Foruwa, will you not dance?' asked the Queen Mother.

Foruwa opened her lips and this was all she said. 'I do not find him here.'

'Who? Who do you not find, daughter?'

'He with whom I wish to create new life. He is not here, Mother. These men's faces are empty; there is nothing in them, nothing at all.'

'What will become of you, my daughter?'

'The day I find him, Mother, the day I find the man, I shall come running to let you know.'

That evening there was heard a new song in the village:

> 'There was a woman long ago,
> Tell that maid, tell that maid;
> There was a woman long ago,
> Who said she would not wed Kwesi,
> She would not marry Shaw,

She would not, would not, would not.
One day she hurried home,
I've found the man, the man, the man,
Tell that maid, tell that maid,
Her man looked like a chief,
Most splendid to behold.
But he turned into a python,
He turned into a python
And swallowed the maid whole.'

From then on there were some in the village who turned their backs on Foruwa as she passed.

But a day came when Foruwa came running to her mother. She burst through the courtyard gate, and there she stood breathless in the yard, full of joy. And a stranger walked in after her and stood beside her, tall and strong as a pillar.

'Here he is, Mother, here is the man.'

The Queen Mother took a slow look at the stranger standing there as strong as a forest tree, and said, 'You bear the light of wisdom on your face, my son. You are welcome. But tell me who you are?'

'Greetings, Mother,' said the stranger. 'I am a worker. My hands are all I have to offer, for they are all my wealth. I have journeyed to see how folk work in other lands. I have that knowledge and my strength. Together, Foruwa and I will build our lives. That is my story.'

Strange as the story is, the stranger was given in marriage to Foruwa.

Soon, quite soon, the people of Kyerefaso began to take notice of Foruwa and the stranger in quite a different way.

'See them work together,' some said. 'They who mingle sweat and song, they for whom toil is joy and life is full and abundant.'

'See,' said others, 'what a harvest the land yields under their care.'

'They have taken the earth and moulded it into bricks. See what a home they have built and how it graces the village.'

'Look at the craft of their fingers – the baskets and kente cloth, the stools and mats – together they make them all.'

'And our children crowd about them, gazing at them with wonder and delight.'

Then it did not satisfy them any more to sit all day at their games beneath the mango trees.

'See what Foruwa and her husband have done together,' they declared. 'Shall the daughters and sons of the land not do the same?'

And soon they too were toiling and their fields began to yield as never before. A new spirit stirred the village. The unkempt houses disappeared one by one and new homes were built after Foruwa's and the stranger's appeared. It seemed as if the village of Kyerefaso had been born anew.

The people themselves became more alive and a new pride possessed them. They were no longer just grabbing from the land what they desired for their comfort and for their stomach's hunger. They were looking at the land with new eyes, feeling it in their blood, and building a beautiful place for themselves and their children. And they did it all, women and men, together.

'Osee!' sang the villagers.

It was festival time again.

'Osee! we are the creators. We shall build a new life with our strength. We shall create it with our minds.'

Following the men and the women came the children. On their heads they carried every kind of produce that the land had yielded and the crafts their fingers had made. Green plantains and yellow bananas were carried by the bunch in large white wooden trays. Garden eggs, tomatoes, red oil-palm nuts warmed by the sun were piled high in black earthen vessels. Oranges, yams and maize filled shining brass trays and golden calabashes. Girls and boys were proudly carrying coloured mats and baskets, and toys that they had made themselves.

The Queen Mother watched the procession gathering on the village square, now emerald green from recent rains. She watched the people moving in a happy dance towards her as she stood outside her house.

She saw Foruwa. Her pile·of charcoal in a large brass tray,

adorned with red hibiscus, danced and swayed with her body. Happiness filled the Queen Mother when she saw her daughter thus.

Then she saw Foruwa's husband. He was carrying a white lamb in his arms, and he was singing happily with the other men and women. The Queen Mother looked on him with pride.

The procession now approached the royal house.

'See how she stands waiting, our Queen Mother. Spread the skins of gentle sheep before her, gently, gently. Spread the yield of the land before her. Spread the craft of your hands before her, gently, gently. Spread the fruit of men's and women's work together at her feet.

'For she is life.'

Three Strong Women

A story from Japan

Long ago, in Japan, there lived a famous wrestler, and he was on his way to the capital city to wrestle before the Emperor.

He strode down the road on legs thick as the trunks of small trees. He had been walking for seven hours and could, and probably would, walk for seven more without getting tired.

The time was autumn, the sky was a cold, watery blue, the air chilly. In the small bright sun, the trees along the roadside glowed red and orange.

The wrestler hummed to himself, 'Zun-zun-zun,' in time with the long swing of his legs. Wind blew through his thin brown robe, and he wore no sword at his side. He felt proud that he needed no sword, even in the darkest and loneliest places. The icy air on his body only reminded him that few tailors would have been able to make expensive warm clothes for a man so broad and tall. He felt much as a wrestler should – strong, healthy, and rather conceited.

A soft roar of fast-moving water beyond the trees told him that he was passing above a river bank. He 'zun-zunned' louder; he loved the sound of his voice and wanted it to sound clearly above the rushing water.

He thought: They call me Forever-Mountain because I am such a good strong wrestler – big, too. I'm a fine, brave man and far too

59

modest ever to say so ...

Just then he saw a girl who must have come up from the river, for she steadied a bucket on her head.

Her hands on the bucket were small, and there was a dimple on each thumb, just below the knuckle. She was a round little girl with red cheeks and a nose like a friendly button. Her eyes looked as though she were thinking of ten thousand funny stories at once. She clambered up onto the road and walked ahead of the wrestler, jolly and bounceful.

'If I don't tickle that fat girl, I shall regret it all my life,' said the wrestler under his breath. 'She's sure to go "squeak" and I shall laugh and laugh. If she drops her bucket, that will be even funnier – and I can always run and fill it again and even carry it home for her.'

He tiptoed up and poked her lightly in the ribs with one huge finger.

'Kochokochokocho!' he said, a fine, ticklish sound in Japanese.

The girl gave a satisfying squeal, giggled, and brought one arm down so that the wrestler's hand was caught between it and her body.

'Ho-ho-ho! You've caught me! I can't move at all!' said the wrestler, laughing.

'I know,' said the jolly girl.

He felt that it was very good-tempered of her to take a joke so well, and started to pull his hand free.

Somehow, he could not.

He tried again, using a little more strength.

'Now, now – let me go, little girl,' he said. 'I am a very powerful man. If I pull too hard I might hurt you.'

'Pull,' said the girl. 'I admire powerful men.'

She began to walk, and though the wrestler tugged and pulled until his feet dug great furrows in the ground, he had to follow. She couldn't have paid him less attention if he had been a puppy – a small one.

Ten minutes later, still tugging while trudging helplessly after her, he was glad that the road was lonely and no one was there to see.

'Please let me go,' he pleaded. 'I am the famous wrestler Forever-Mountain. I must go and show my strength before the Emperor' – he burst out weeping from shame and confusion – 'and you're hurting my hand!'

The girl steadied the bucket on her head with her free hand and dimpled sympathetically over her shoulder. 'You poor, sweet little Forever-Mountain,' she said. 'Are you tired? Shall I carry you? I can leave the water here and come back for it later.'

'I do not want you to carry me. I want you to let me go, and then I want to forget I ever saw you. What do you want with me?' moaned the pitiful wrestler.

'I only want to help you,' said the girl, now pulling him steadily up and up a narrow mountain path. 'Oh, I am sure you'll have no more trouble than anyone else when you come up against the other wrestlers. You'll win, or else you'll lose, and you won't be too badly hurt either way. But aren't you afraid you might meet a really *strong* man someday?'

Forever-Mountain turned white. He stumbled. He was imagining being laughed at throughout Japan as 'Hardly-Ever-Mountain'.

She glanced back.

'You see? Tired already,' she said. 'I'll walk more slowly. Why don't you come along to my mother's house and let us make a strong man of you? The wrestling in the capital isn't due to begin for three months. I know, because Grandmother thought she'd go. You'd be spending all that time in bad company and wasting what little power you have.'

'All right. Three months. I'll come along,' said the wrestler. He felt he had nothing more to lose. Also, he feared that the girl might become angry if he refused, and place him in the top of a tree until he changed his mind.

'Fine,' she said happily. 'We are almost there.'

She freed his hand. It had become red and a little swollen. 'But if you break your promise and run off, I shall have to chase you and carry you back.'

Soon they arrived in a small valley. A simple farmhouse with a

'Please let me go,' he pleaded

thatched roof stood in the middle.

'Grandmother is at home, but she is an old lady and she's probably sleeping.' The girl shaded her eyes with one hand. 'But Mother should be bringing our cow back from the field – oh, there's Mother now!'

She waved. The woman coming around the corner of the house put down the cow she was carrying and waved back.

She smiled and came across the grass, walking with a lively bounce like her daughter's. Well, maybe her bounce was a little more solid, thought the wrestler.

'Excuse me,' she said, brushing some cow hair from her dress and dimpling, also like her daughter. 'These mountain paths are full of stones. They hurt the cow's feet. And who is the nice young man you've brought, Maru-me?'

The girl explained. 'And we have only three months!' she finished anxiously.

'Well, it's not long enough to do much, but it's not so short a time that we can't do something,' said her mother, looking thoughtful. 'But he does look terribly feeble. He'll need a lot of good things to eat. Maybe when he gets stronger he can help Grandmother with some of the easy work about the house.'

'That will be fine!' said the girl, and she called her grandmother – loudly, for the old lady was a little deaf.

'I'm coming!' came a creaky voice from inside the house, and a little old woman leaning on a stick and looking very sleepy tottered out of the door. As she came towards them she stumbled over the roots of a great oak tree.

'Heh! My eyes aren't what they used to be. That's the fourth time this month I've stumbled over that tree,' she complained and, wrapping her skinny arms about its trunk, pulled it out of the ground.

'Oh, Grandmother! You should have let me pull it up for you,' said Maru-me.

'Hm. I hope I didn't hurt my poor old back,' muttered the old lady. She called out, 'Daughter! Throw that tree away like a good girl, so no one will fall over it. But make sure it doesn't hit anybody.'

'You can help Mother with the tree,' Maru-me said to Forever-Mountain. 'On second thoughts, you'd better not help. Just watch.'

Her mother went to the tree, picked it up in her two hands and threw it – clumsily and with a little gasp. Up went the tree, sailing end over end, growing smaller and smaller as it flew. It landed with a faint crash far up the mountainside.

'Ah, how clumsy,' she said. 'I meant to throw it *over* the mountain. It's probably blocking the path now, and I'll have to get up early tomorrow to move it.'

The wrestler was not listening. He had very quietly fainted.

'Oh! We must put him to bed,' said Maru-me.

'Poor, feeble young man,' said her mother.

'I hope we can do something for him. Here, let me carry him, he's light,' said the grandmother. She slung him over her shoulder and carried him into the house, creaking along with her cane.

The next day they began the work of making Forever-Mountain into what they thought a strong man should be. They gave him the simplest food to eat, and the toughest. Day by day they prepared his rice with less and less water, until no ordinary man could have chewed or digested it.

Every day he was made to do the work of five men, and every evening he wrestled with Grandmother. Maru-me and her mother agreed that Grandmother, being old and feeble, was the least likely to injure him accidentally. They hoped the exercise might be good for the old lady's rheumatism.

He grew stronger and stronger but was hardly aware of it. Grandmother could still throw him easily into the air – and catch him again – without ever changing her sweet old smile.

He quite forgot that outside this valley he was one of the greatest wrestlers in Japan and was called Forever-Mountain. His legs had been like logs; now they were like pillars. His big hands were hard as stones, and when he cracked his knuckles the sound was like trees splitting on a cold night.

Sometimes he did an exercise that wrestlers do in Japan – raising one foot high above the ground and bringing it down with a crash. Then people in nearby villages looked up at the winter sky and told one another that it was very late in the year for thunder.

Soon he could pull up a tree as well as the grandmother. He could even throw one – but only a small distance. One evening, near the end of his third month, he wrestled with Grandmother and held her down for half a minute.

'Heh-heh!' She chortled and got up, smiling with every wrinkle. 'I would never have believed it!'

Maru-me squealed with joy and threw her arms around him – gently, for she was afraid of cracking his ribs.

'Very good, very good! What a strong man,' said her mother, who had just come home from the fields, carrying, as usual, the cow. She put the cow down and patted the wrestler on the back.

They agreed that he was now ready to show some *real* strength before the Emperor.

'Take the cow along with you tomorrow when you go,' said the mother. 'Sell her and buy yourself a belt – a silken belt. Buy the fattest and heaviest one you can find. Wear it when you appear before the Emperor, as a souvenir from us.'

'I wouldn't think of taking your only cow. You've already done too much for me. And you'll need her to plough the fields, won't you?'

They burst out laughing, Maru-me squealed, her mother roared. The grandmother cackled so hard and long that she choked and had to be pounded on the back.

'Oh, dear,' said the mother, still laughing. 'You didn't think we used our cow for anything like *work*! Why, Grandmother here is stronger than five cows!'

'The cow is our pet.' Maru-me giggled. 'She has lovely brown eyes.'

'But it really gets tiresome having to carry her back and forth each day so that she has enough grass to eat,' said her mother.

'Then you must let me give you all the prize money that I win,' said Forever-Mountain.

'Oh, no! We wouldn't think of it!' said Maru-me. 'Because we all like you too much to sell you anything. And it is not proper to accept gifts of money from strangers.'

'True,' said Forever-Mountain. 'I will now ask your mother's and grandmother's permission to marry you. I want to be one of the family.'

'Oh! I'll get a wedding dress ready!' said Maru-me.

The mother and grandmother pretended to consider very seriously, but they quickly agreed.

Next morning Forever-Mountain tied his hair up in the topknot that all Japanese wrestlers wear, and got ready to leave. He thanked Maru-me and her mother and bowed very low to the grandmother, since she was the oldest and had been a fine wrestling partner.

Then he picked up the cow in his arms and trudged up the mountain. When he reached the top, he slung the cow over one shoulder and waved goodbye to Maru-me.

At the first town he came to, Forever-Mountain sold the cow. She brought a good price because she was unusually fat from never having worked in her life. With the money, he bought the heaviest silken belt he could find.

When he reached the palace grounds, many of the other wrestlers were already there, sitting about, eating enormous bowls of rice, comparing one another's weight and telling stories. They paid little attention to Forever-Mountain, except to wonder why he had arrived so late this year. Some of them noticed that he had grown very quiet and took no part at all in their boasting.

All the ladies and gentlemen of the court were waiting in a special courtyard for the wrestling to begin. They wore many robes, one on top of another, heavy with embroidery and gold cloth, and sweat ran down their faces and froze in the winter afternoon. The gentlemen had long swords so weighted with gold and precious stones that they could never have used them, even if they had known how. The court ladies, with their long black hair hanging down behind, had their faces painted dead white, which made them look frightened. They had pulled out their real eyebrows and painted new ones high above the place where eyebrows are supposed to be, and this made them all look as though they were very surprised at something.

Behind a screen sat the Emperor – by himself, because he was too noble for ordinary people to look at. He was a lonely old man with a kind, tired face. He hoped the wrestling would end quickly so that he could go to his room and write poems.

The first two wrestlers chosen to fight were Forever-Mountain and a wrestler who was said to have the biggest stomach in the country. He and Forever-Mountain both threw some salt into the ring. It was understood that this drove away evil spirits.

Then the other wrestler, moving his stomach somewhat out of the way, raised his foot and brought it down with a fearful stamp. He glared fiercely at Forever-Mountain as if to say, 'Now *you* stamp, you poor frightened man!'

Forever-Mountain raised his foot. He brought it down.

There was a sound like thunder, the earth shook, and the other wrestler bounced into the air and out of the ring, as gracefully as any soap bubble.

He picked himself up and bowed to the Emperor's screen.

'The earth god is angry. Possibly there is something the matter with the salt,' he said. 'I do not think I shall wrestle this season.' And he walked out, looking very suspiciously over one shoulder at Forever-Mountain.

Five other wrestlers then and there decided that they were not wrestling this season, either. They all looked annoyed with Forever-Mountain.

From then on, Forever-Mountain brought his foot down lightly. As each wrestler came into the ring, he picked him up very gently, carried him out, and placed him before the Emperor's screen, bowing most courteously every time.

The court ladies' eyebrows went up even higher. The gentlemen looked disturbed and a little afraid. They loved to see fierce, strong men tugging and grunting at each other, but Forever-Mountain was a little too much for them. Only the Emperor was happy behind his screen, for now, with the wrestling over so quickly, he would have that much more time to write his poems. He ordered all the prize money handed over to Forever-Mountain.

'But,' he said, 'you had better not wrestle any more.' He stuck a finger through his screen and waggled it at the other wrestlers, who were sitting on the ground weeping with disappointment like great fat babies.

Forever-Mountain promised not to wrestle any more. Everybody looked relieved. The wrestlers sitting on the ground almost smiled.

'I think I shall become a farmer,' Forever-Mountain said, and left at once to go back to Maru-me.

Maru-me was waiting for him. When she saw him coming, she ran down the mountain, picked him up, together with the heavy bags of prize money, and carried him halfway up the mountainside. Then she giggled and put him down. The rest of the way she let him carry her.

Forever-Mountain kept his promise to the Emperor and never fought in public again. His name was forgotten in the capital. But up in the mountains, sometimes, the earth shakes and rumbles, and they say that is Forever-Mountain and Maru-me's grandmother practising wrestling in the hidden valley.

Claus Stamm

The Wonderful Pearl

A story from Vietnam

Once upon a time there was an orphan girl called Wa, who lived on the banks of the Mekong River. Ever since she had been a little girl and could carry a basketful of rice upon her back, she had worked for the village headman.

Like the other villagers, she toiled long and hard for her master, and was hardly given enough to eat in return. She had to cut down the biggest trees that even the strongest men could barely fell. And when the rice was ripe, she had to peel the husks from dawn till dusk. Her hands were always blistered from cutting wood, and when the skin had hardened, her palms would itch from the coarse rice husks. Each night she would gather herbs to put on her raw, itching hands, and other workers would come to her for their wounds to be soothed – for she had a great knowledge of wild plants and their healing powers.

One day she was cleaning the new harvest of rice with her friend, Ho. Ho was so thin that his ribs stuck through his tattered shirt. As they worked they spoke of the drudgery of their lives and wondered, sadly, how many of their people would die of starvation before the year was out.

Before long, the headman's messenger arrived and ordered Wa to guard the rice house which stood on piles close by the paddy field.

The rice house was filled to the roof with stores of rice, and the hungry girl longed to eat some, but she was ever mindful of the master's warning.

'An evil spirit protects my rice. If you eat even one grain, the spirit will jump inside you. Then you will die and turn into a grain of rice!'

In her fear, poor Wa went hungry.

As darkness came, Wa was overcome with tiredness and she fell asleep. In her dreams she saw her master growing fat and rich from the store of rice, which grew bigger and bigger from the toil of her fellow villagers, while they grew thin and sick.

All of a sudden, she was rudely awakened by a vicious kick in her side. It was the headman's son. 'You lazy pig!' he screamed in her ear. 'Fill this pail with water by my return.'

Wa jumped up in alarm as he went laughing on his way. She took the pail and ran swiftly to the river to fill it up.

The waters of the river were ruffled by a gentle breeze as they lapped softly at the girl's sore and aching feet. She sighed and bent down to fill the pail. All of a sudden, the waters began to foam and ring out like the torong's* twanging strings, making her scamper back to dry land in fear.

Out of the silver foam appeared a maiden, tall and proud, wearing a long shimmering dress. She approached Wa and, taking her trembling hand, softly said, 'The Water Spirit's young daughter has fallen ill. And our sprites say that you, Wa, are wise with herbs and can cure her. Come with me and see the girl.'

'No, no, I cannot,' Wa cried out. 'I have to guard the rice house. The master would kill me if he should find me gone.'

'Do not anger us, Wa. The Water Spirit is mightier even than your village chief. If you do not come, the sprites will punish you.'

A dry pathway suddenly opened before her and the stately maid led Wa down into the underwater depths.

Wa was told that the Water Spirit's daughter had had a scorpion sting while playing on the shore. Ever since she had been ill. All the underwater doctors – the shrimps and eels – were fussing about the

* An instrument made from split bamboo cane.

70

Out of the silver foam appeared a maiden

poor sick girl, but none could cure the strange sickness that had overcome her. For three months she had lain in a fever, unable to eat or sleep.

Wa gently touched the wound and told the sprites what herbs they should collect. When these were ready, she used them on the girl, and three days later she was well.

The Water Spirit was overjoyed. 'Dear Wa,' he said, 'what will you take as reward?'

'My only wish is to save my people from need,' Wa replied.

Thereupon, the Spirit handed her a precious pearl, saying, 'This pearl will make any wish come true.'

Wa thanked the Water Spirit and returned to dry land along the underwater path. When she reached the rice house, she saw in horror the tracks of birds, big and small, all around it. They had helped themselves to half the unprotected rice!

An old man passed by just then, and stared at Wa in surprise. 'Where did you get to, Wa, these past three months?' he said. 'Be warned, for you're in trouble. Just look about you: those thieving birds have stolen the master's rice. He is searching for you and his rage is terrible.'

Wa went sadly on her way. Eventually she sat down on the ground and hung her head in woe. Her thin dress became quite wet with tears. And then, all at once, she remembered the precious pearl. Taking out the Spirit's gift, she murmured, 'Pearl, wonderful pearl, bring me rice to eat.'

Right away, a huge bamboo dish of rice appeared before her, filled with all manner of tasty food. And at her back a store of rice grew up three times higher than the master's rice house.

She clapped her hands with joy and began to eat to her heart's content. Yet suddenly she stopped. Her thoughts were of her dear friend Ho. He too was poor and had to toil in the master's paddy fields all day. So she took out the pearl again and said, 'Pearl, wonderful pearl, bring me a house, a pair of oxen and some hens. And then bring my friend Ho to me.'

Hardly had Wa spoken than, to her right, a tall house on bamboo stilts grew up, with hens scratching round about; and there beneath it was a pair of milk-white oxen. Inside the house she saw gongs and copper pans, a brass kettle on a stove and jars of sweets. Just then an astonished Ho appeared and together they walked into the house as Wa told him her wonderful story.

Next morning Wa made her way to the headman's house. As soon as he set eyes on the girl, he roared like a stricken ox.

'Ahrr-rrr, here comes the lump of oxen dung, the one who stole my rice. I'll have her fed to the tigers in the hills!'

'It was not my fault you lost your rice,' Wa spoke up boldly. 'No matter, I'll make up what you lost; just send your son to collect it.'

'Lead on,' snarled the headman's son. 'I'll take it now. And if you fail by a single grain I'll bring your head back on a tray.'

When the son set eyes on Wa's rich house, his mouth dropped open in surprise and his eyes grew wide like a bullock's.

'Hey there, Ho!' shouted Wa. 'The master's son has come for rice. Give him all he wants. I'm going to the river to fish.'

When the man recovered from his shock, he hurried down to the riverbank and stared at the girl with fresh respect. He thought that she looked stronger and sturdier than the finest jungle tree.

'I do n-n-not want your r-r-rice, dear Wa,' he stammered. 'I wish to m-m-marry you.'

Wa only laughed. 'Take your rice and go,' she said. 'I cannot stand the sight of you.'

Slowly he made his way back home and reported all to his father. In a rage, the headman called his guards.

'Gather up your spears, your swords, your bows and arrows,' he yelled. 'We go to slay that low-born girl and take her riches for ourselves.'

But the good people of the village ran swiftly to warn Wa of the master's plans. At once, the bold young girl took out the magic pearl and said, 'Pearl, wonderful pearl, protect us from this evil man.'

Suddenly a chain of lofty mountains sprang up around the headman's house. He and his men tried to scale the heights. But after three whole months they had only managed to climb an eighth of the mountain and eventually they had to give up. They were forced to return defeated to their narrow valley and were never able to bother the poor again.

Meanwhile, on the other side of the mountain, Wa and Ho lived in contentment. The wise, just Wa shared out her wealth among the people who never went hungry again, and she protected them always with her wonderful pearl.

The Squire's Bride

An old Norwegian story

There was once a rich squire with a mint of silver in the barn and gold aplenty in the bank. He farmed over hill and dale, was ruddy and stout, yet he lacked a wife. So he had a mind to wed.

After all, since I am rich, he thought, I can pick and choose whatever maid I wish.

One afternoon the squire was wandering down the lane when he spotted a sturdy lass toiling in the hayfield. And he rubbed his grizzled chins, muttering to himself, 'Oh aye, I fancy she'd do all right, and save me a packet on wages too. Since she's poor and humble she'll take my offer, right enough.'

So he had her brought to the manor house where he sat her down, all hot and flustered.

'Now then, gal,' he began, 'I've a mind to take a wife.'

'Mind on then,' she said. 'One may mind of much and more.'

She wondered whether the old buffer had his sights set on her; why else should she be summoned?

'Aye, lass, I've picked thee out. Tha'll make a decent wife, sure enough.'

'No thank you,' said she, 'though much obliged, I'm sure.'

The squire's ruddy face turned ruby red; he was not used to people talking back. The more he blathered, the more she turned him down, and none too politely either. Yet the more she refused, the more he wanted what he could not have. With a final sigh, he dismissed the lass and sent for her father; perhaps the man would talk some sense into his daughter's head.

'Go to it, man,' the squire roared. 'I'll overlook the money you owe me and give you a meadow into the bargain. What d'ye say to that?'

'Oh, aye, Squire. Be sure I'll bring her round,' the father said. 'Pardon her plain speaking; she's young yet and don't know what's best.'

All the same, in spite of all his coaxing and bawling, the girl was adamant – she would not have the old miser even if he were made of gold! And that was that.

When the poor farmer did not return to the manor house with the girl's consent, the squire stormed and stamped impatiently. And next day he went to call on the man.

'Settle this matter right away,' he ranted on, 'or it'll be the worse for you. I won't bide a day longer for my bride.'

There was nothing for it. Together the master and the farmer hatched a plan: the squire was to see to all the wedding chores – parson, guests, wedding feast – and the farmer would send his daughter at the appointed hour. He would say nothing of the wedding to her, but just let her think that work awaited her up at the big house.

Of course, when she arrived she would be so dazzled by the wedding dress, afeared of the parson and awed by the guests that she would readily give her consent. How could a farm girl refuse the squire? And so it was arranged.

When all the guests had assembled at the manor and the white wedding gown laid out and the parson, in black hat and cloak, settled down, the master sent for a stable lad. 'Go to the farmer,' he ordered, 'and bring back what I'm promised. And be back here in two ticks or I'll tan your hide!'

The lad rushed off, wondering what the promise was. In no time at all he was knocking on the farmer's door.

'My master's sent me to fetch what you promised him,' panted the lad.

'Oh, aye, dare say he has,' the farmer said. 'She's down in the meadow; you'd better take her then.'

Off ran the lad to the meadow and found the daughter raking hay.

'I've come to fetch what your father promised the squire,' he said all out of breath.

It did not take the girl long to figure out the plot.

So that's their game, she thought, a twinkle in her eye. 'Right, then, lad, you'd better take her then. It's the old grey mare grazing over there.'

With a leap and a bound the lad was on the grey mare's back and riding home at full gallop. Once there he leapt down at the door, dashed inside and called up to the squire,

'She's at the door now, Squire.'

'Well done,' called down the master. 'Take her up to my old mother's room.'

'But, master –'

'Don't but me, you scoundrel,' the old codger roared. 'If you can't manage her on your own, get someone else to help.'

On glimpsing the squire's angry face he knew it was no use arguing. So he called some farmhands and they set to work. Some pulled the old mare's ears, others pushed her rump; they heaved and shoved until finally they got her up the stairs and into the empty room. There they tied the reins to a bedpost and let her be.

Wiping the sweat from his brow, the lad now reported to the squire.

'That's the darndest job I've ever done,' he complained.

'Now send the wenches up to dress her in the wedding gown,' said the squire.

The stable lad stared.

'Get on with it, dung-head. And tell them not to forget the veil and crown. Jump to it!'

Forthwith the lad burst into the pantry to tell the news.

'Hey, listen here, go upstairs and dress the old mare in wedding

She let out a fierce neigh, turned tail and fled out of the house

clothes. That's what the master says. He must be playing a joke on his guests.'

The cooks and chambermaids all but split their sides with laughter. But in the end they scrambled up the stairs and dressed the poor grey mare as if she were a bride. That done, the lad went off once more to the squire.

'Right, lad, now bring her downstairs. I'll be in the drawing room with my guests. Just throw open the door and announce the bride.'

There came a noisy clatter and thumping on the stairs as the old grey mare was prodded down; at last she stood impatiently in the hallway before the door. Then, all at once, the door burst open and all the guests looked round in expectation.

What a shock they got!

In trotted the old grey mare dressed up as bride, with a crown sprawling on one ear, veil draped over her eyes, and gown covering her rump. Seeing the crowd, she let out a fierce neigh, turned tail and fled out of the house.

The parson spilled his glass of port all down his purple front; the squire gaped in amazement, the guests let out a roar of laughter that could be heard for miles around.

And the squire, they say, never went courting again.

As for the girl, some say she married, some say not. It matters little. What is certain is that she lived happily ever after.

The Aztec Sun Goddess
An Aztec tale

Before the Sun that now shines brightly on the land came into being, there had been other suns: four in all. Each died away in turn before our present Sun appeared.

After the fourth sun, the earth was plunged in gloom: it had no dawn, no dusk, no sunlit days. So the gods resolved to give the world a fifth and final sun. They assembled at Tectihuacan, Place of the Gods, and argued loud and long as to what should happen. Finally it was decided.

Since the first four suns had died, either because they had grown tired of shining all day long, or because the gods had grown jealous of constant sunshine that outshone them, there had to be a change. The gods themselves would create a sun and a moon. That way, the Sun would shine for only half the day, and moonlight would light the heavens while the Sun was at rest.

But who would be the Sun and the Moon?

It had to be two gods without the power to retake their godlike form. Therefore, the gods decreed that there would be a sacrifice: whoever volunteered would not live to see themselves as Sun or Moon, but would change their form so that the Sun and Moon would last for ever.

Only one god came forward: Tecuciztecatl, God of Snails and

Worms. He was rich and strong and vain. He thought that by sacrificing himself he would gain immortal glory as the brilliant Sun.

No one wished to be the Moon. Uneasily the gods looked about them. At last their gaze fell upon a humble goddess in their midst: Nanahuaztzin, the little leper. If she agreed, the gods declared, they would remove her sores and ugly form for ever and turn her into the Moon.

Nanahuaztzin did not wish to die. Yet she smiled happily when she thought of how she would bring people light to guide them on their way.

The gods began their preparations. Two tall stone altars with wide flights of steps were built: one for the Sun and one for the Moon – though which was which had yet to be agreed. Both sacrifices were bathed and dressed in their own way.

Tecuciztecatl put on a fine plumage and brightly coloured robes, earrings of turquoise and jade, and a collar of shining gold.

Nanahuaztzin, the little leper, had no such finery. So she daubed her red-raw body white and donned a thin, torn paper dress through which her puny frame showed.

Meanwhile, upon the altars, the gods had built a sacrificial pyre. So many logs of wood were heaped upon it that the heavens seemed to light up in the roaring blaze. At this spectacle, Tecuciztecatl trembled in fear and bit his lip; yet Nanahuaztzin sat quietly by, her hands folded in her lap.

Tecuciztecatl was honoured to be first to leap into the flames. At the gods' command, he drew near the pyre and stood tall and grand upon his altar of white stone, his plume of red and green and yellow streaming in the wind. But his courage failed him and he drew back abruptly, pale and trembling. Three times he was summoned, and three times he nervously withdrew.

The gods finally lost patience and turned to little Nanahuaztzin, shouting, 'Jump!'

She stepped forward instantly and stood unflinching on the altar's edge. Then she closed her eyes, smiled bravely as she thought of her sacrifice, and leapt into the red heart of the flames.

Never was the dawn so beautiful

Angry and ashamed – but more afraid that the noble power of the Sun would not be his – Tecuciztecatl shut tight his eyes and jumped. But his leap was to the side, where the fire was weakest and the ash was thick.

Just at that moment an eagle swooped from nowhere into the flames, then out again so quickly that only his wingtips were singed. He flew upwards swiftly with a bright ball of fire in his beak – like a fiery arrow through the sky – until he reached the eastern gates of Tectihuacan. There he left the ball of fire – for thus little Nanahuaztzin had become – and she took her seat upon a throne of billowing clouds. She had shining golden tresses strung with pearls and precious shells, all shimmering in the mists of dawn; and her lips were brightest scarlet.

Never was the dawn so beautiful. A great roar of pleasure issued from the gods and rumbled through the morning sky.

Just at that moment a hawk swooped into the burning embers of the fire and was scorched a charcoal black. At once the hawk emerged with a glowing, ash-coloured ball of fire held in its beak. And this it bore to the sky to set some way from the Sun.

Thus the cowardly Tecuciztecatl, God of Snails, became the Moon.

In their anger at the feeble Moon, the gods cast sticks and stones up at his pale face. One flung a rabbit – the nearest thing to hand. It flew straight and true, striking the Moon full in the face.

Ever since, when the Moon is full, you may see the scars left by the rabbit's long ears and flying feet.

Thereafter, as the Sun makes her journey round the world, bringing warmth and light, the Moon sets off in vain pursuit. But he is always slow to start. And when, cold and weary, he reaches the west, the Sun has long since set, and his once fine robes have turned to tatters.

That is the story of the fifth and final Sun.

'The Sun and the Moon'

The Sun is filled with shining light,
It blazes far and wide.
The Moon reflects the sunlight back
But has no light inside.

I think I'd rather be the Sun
That shines so bold and bright
Than be the Moon, that only glows
With someone else's light.

Elaine Daron

Further Reading

I have found *very few* books I would recommend unreservedly – some are full of princesses, even spirited ones; some of witches; some of stepmothers; some have marriage as the ultimate ideal; and so on. The following (all American) provide a pleasant change:

Alison Lurie, *Clever Gretchen and Other Forgotten Folktales*, Thomas Y. Crowell, New York, 1980

Rosemary Minard (ed.), *Womenfolk and Fairy Tales*, Houghton Mifflin Co., Boston, 1975

Ethel Johnston Phelps, *Tatterhood and Other Tales*, Feminist Press, New York, 1978; *The Maid of the North: Feminist Folk Tales from Around the World*, Holt, Rinehart & Winston, New York, 1980

Nancy Schimmel, *Just Enough to Make a Story*, Sisters' Choice Press, Berkeley, 1982

Marlo Thomas, *Free To Be ... You and Me*, Ms Foundation, McGraw-Hill, New York, 1974

The following books have helped to open my eyes:

Elena Belotti, *Little Girls*, Writers and Readers Publishing Cooperative, 1975

Bob Dixon, *Catching Them Young: Sex, Race and Class in Children's Fiction*, Pluto Press, 1979

Andrea Dworkin, *Woman Hating*, E. P. Dutton, 1974

Madonna Kolbenschlag, *Kiss Sleeping Beauty Good-bye*, Doubleday & Co.

Inc., New York, 1979

Susan Sharpe. *Just Like a Girl*, Penguin, 1976

Judith Stinton (ed.), *Racism and Sexism in Children's Books*, Writers and Readers Publishing Cooperative, 1979

Rosemary Stones and Andrew Mann, *Spare Rib List of Non-Sexist Children's Books*, Spare Rib, 1979

Sexism in Children's Books, Writers and Readers Publishing Cooperative, 1976

Jack Zipes, *Breaking the Magic Spell*, Heinemann, 1979; *Fairy Tales and the Art of Subversion*, Heinemann, 1983; *The Trials and Tribulations of Little Red Riding Hood*, Heinemann, 1983

Sources

'The Woman in the Moon' is retold from Ella Elizabeth Clark, *Indian Legends of Canada*, McClelland & Stewart, Toronto, 1960

'A Mother's Yarn' was collected near Murmansk in 1977; a version may be found in *Khozyaika travy: saamskie skazki*, Sovetskaya Rossiya, Murmansk, 1973

'The Nagging Husband' 'wanders' all over Eastern Europe; this version comes from Estonia: *Skazki yantarnovo morya*, Eesti Raamat, Tallin, 1968

'Gulnara the Tartar Warrior' was collected in the hamlet of Verkhnyeye Yarkeyevo, Bashkiria, in 1968

'Caterina the Wise' is translated from Italo Calvino, *Fiabe Italiane*, Giulio Einaudi editore, Turin, 1959

'Oona and the Giant Cuchulain' is retold from a tale by Ruth Manning Sanders from *Folk and Fairy Tales*, Methuen, 1978

'Aina-kizz and the Black-Bearded Bai' was collected near Alma-Ata, Kazakhstan, in 1964; a version may be found in *Chudesny sad. Kazakhskie narodnye skazki*, Detskaya Literatura, Leningrad, 1970

'A Pottle o' Brains' comes partly from the old English tale 'Coat o' Clay', collected by Mrs Balfour (*Folk-Lore*, I, 1890), and partly from 'A Pottle o' Brains', published by Joseph Jacobs in *English Fairy Tales*, Bodley Head, 1968

'The Maid Who Chose a Husband' is retold from a tale by Efua Sutherland, 'New Life at Kyerefaso', from Richard Rive (ed.), *Modern African Prose*, Heinemann, 1964

'Three Strong Women' is reproduced from Claus Stamm, *Three Strong Women*, Viking Press, New York, 1962

'The Wonderful Pearl' is translated from *Contes d'Indochine*, Gallimard, Paris, 1980

'The Squire's Bride' is retold from P. C. Asbjörnsen and Jörgen E. Moe, *A Collection of Popular Tales from the Norse*, Norroena Society, Oslo, 1907

'The Aztec Sun Goddess' is retold from Carleton Beals, *Stories Told by the Aztecs before the Spaniards Came*, Abelard-Schuman, New York, 1970

'The Sun and the Moon', by Elaine Daron, from Marlo Thomas, *Free To Be ... You and Me*, Ms Foundation, McGraw-Hill, New York, 1974

Note: Apart from the tale from Japan, the retelling and translations are my own.